"TAKE OUT YOUR PISTOL!"

"No," Train gasped. "You'll kill me."

"I'm gonna kill you anyway, scum!" Trapp shouted. "Take it out!"

"Why are you doing this?" Train said desperately. "She was just a squaw."

"Maybe," Trapp said, removing the pistol from his belt, "but she was *my* squaw."

"Who are you?"

"Trapp," John Henry said, "the man who killed you. Now take out your pistol and die like a man, or get down on your knees and die like a coward. Your choice."

To his credit—and Trapp's relief—Train reacted angrily.

"Damn you!" the young man called, and drew his pistol....

TRAPP'S MOUNTAIN

ROBERT J. RANDISI

LEISURE BOOKS NEW YORK CITY

A LEISURE BOOK®

August 2005

Published by

Dorchester Publishing Co., Inc.
200 Madison Avenue
New York, NY 10016

Originally published under the title *Mountain Man's Vengeance*.

ISBN 0-8439-5340-3

Printed in the United States of America.

Visit us on the web at www.dorchesterpub.com.

TRAPP'S MOUNTAIN

PROLOGUE

1

Green River, 1846

John Henry Trapp came down from the Green River country with killing on his mind.

Trapp was thirty-nine years old at that point of his life, and was coming off the happiest year of his life. The reason for that had been White Dove. He had found the Crow squaw hurt and frozen a year ago, and had taken her back to his hut with him. He'd nursed her back to health, and since then they had been living together.

Until a week ago.

He had gone downriver to set some new traps and check the old ones. He'd been gone two days, and when he returned, his hut was gone, burned to the ground. Everything he owned that he hadn't had with him had burned with it.

In the rubble he found White Dove—what was left of her. He had picked up her charred, scorched body in his arms and carried her away from the hut. He spent hours digging in the hard ground until he had a deep-enough grave and then laid her in it and covered her up. After that he mounted up and started tracking the men who had killed her.

Their trail led him down from the mountain.

He had no way of knowing that he would not see that mountain again for twenty-five years.

2

Huntsville Prison, Texas, 1871

When John Henry Trapp walked through the front gates of Huntsville Prison—*out*, not in—the first thing he did was look at the sky.

It looked different.

It looked different from the piece of sky he'd been able to see from the window of his cell. It looked cleaner, bigger . . . freer.

But it still didn't look like the sky he could see from the Rockies.

For the first five years he'd been in jail, all he could think of was White Dove.

After ten years he found that he'd forgotten what

White Dove looked like—but he had never forgotten that Rocky Mountain sky.

Now that he was out, there was nothing he wanted more than to see it again.

He was wearing clothes they had given him, had five dollars in his pocket that they had given him. There was a horse waiting for him—not much of a horse, but then they'd given him *that*, too.

All he had that was his was his old Sharps. A guard, a man who loved guns, had taken care of it for him, kept it in good working order, and had given it back to him. The guard, a man named Connors, had started working there the same time Trapp had been brought there, and had promised to care for the weapon.

To Trapp's surprise, he had kept his promise. It was the only decent thing that had happened to Trapp in the last twenty-five years.

"You're getting out," Connors said to him as he handed him the Sharps. "I'll be here until I die. Ain't much I can do about that."

"You could leave, too," Trapp said.

"And go where?"

"To the mountains."

"You go to your mountain, Trapp," Connors said, shaking his head. "Don't stop for nothing until you get there, ya hear?"

"I hear."

They shook hands.

That was when Trapp went outside and looked up at the sky.

3

Now he walked to the flea-bitten nag they had given him and mounted up.

That was okay.

He was pretty flea-bitten himself.

He was sixty-four years old.

BOOK ONE

BACK TO THE WORLD

ONE

Fry rode into Littlesworth, Texas, hungry enough to eat a bear.

He stabled his horse and went directly to the saloon. He'd find himself a hotel room after he saw to the inner man.

He entered the Lucky Star Saloon, approached the bar, and immediately helped himself to one of the hard-boiled eggs that were piled up in a bowl. Next to the bowl was a sign that said *FREE*.

"Hey!" the bartender said.

Fry looked at the man, still holding an egg in his left hand.

"What?"

"Those are for paying customers."

Fry looked at the sign to see if he'd read it correctly.

"Don't that say free?"

"It does," the bartender said, "but it means free with a drink."

"Why don't it say free with a drink then?"

The bartender, a rangy man with big shoulders and hands, leaned forward and said, "Are you lookin' for trouble, son?"

Fry was twenty-five, but he knew he had to live with looking younger, and sometimes getting treated that way.

"No, sir," Fry said, "I'm looking for a drink to go with this egg."

"What'll you have?"

"Beer."

"Comin' up."

Fry rolled the egg on the bar top while waiting for his beer, then began to peel it. When the bartender set his beer down in front of him, he took a bite of the egg and washed it down with a deep swallow of beer.

"You payin' for the beer?" the bartender asked.

"Of course I'm paying," Fry said, digging into his pocket. "What do I look like, a deadbeat?"

The bartender didn't comment. He just kept looking at Fry until a coin hit the bar top. It bounced once and the bartender caught it with a quick, practiced motion.

"One drink," he told Fry, "one egg."

As the man turned away, Fry made a face at him and quickly snatched another egg, pushing it into his vest pocket. He picked up his beer then and walked to a table at the rear of the room. It was early and there were only three or four other people in the place. The gaming tables were covered, and there were not yet any women working the place.

Fry had enough money for another beer, one night

in the hotel, and then he had to pick between a meal or a woman.

For a man who had been on the trail as long as he had, it was a difficult choice.

When Trapp rode into Littlesworth that afternoon, he attracted attention. He had always attracted attention wherever he went because he was such a big man. Now he still had the height he'd always had, but there was a lot less meat on his bones. When he'd gone into prison, he'd had huge shoulders, a deep chest, hard biceps, and thighs like tree trunks. Although he was far from emaciated, he was still only a shadow of the strapping young man he'd once been. Add to that that he was riding a half-dead horse and wearing ill-fitting clothes, and he would have been a curiosity anywhere he went.

He rode to the livery and the liveryman cast a critical eye over him and the horse.

"What do you want me to do with him?" the man asked. "Bury him?"

"Just give him some feed," Trapp said.

"A waste of good feed, if you ask me."

"I didn't," Trapp said, fixing the man with a hard stare.

The man met Trapp's eyes for only a moment, then he swallowed and looked away.

"Jest makin' a comment, is all," he muttered, walking the horse inside the livery.

Trapp turned and walked toward the center of town. This was the first town he'd been in since being released from prison that morning. It was a small town, but to Trapp it seemed to bustle with activity.

That was because he was still used to the mountains, where if you ran across one other person over the course of a month it was a lot—unless, of course, you went to rendezvous. That was what Trapp missed the most, the mountain man rendezvous, but they were gone even before he went to jail.

As uncomfortable as he was being out among people, he kept his back stiff and walked purposefully, as if he knew exactly where he was going. In point of fact, he had no idea *where* he was going or what he was going to do until he saw the saloon.

He hadn't had a beer in twenty-five years.

Fry was looking over the saloon girls, trying to decide if any of them was worth more than a meal, when the big man entered the saloon. Fry noticed him right away. He noticed the ill fit of his clothes, the prison pallor of his face. He thought that this man must have been a monster ten or twenty years ago, but he still wouldn't want to tangle with him now.

He also noticed the old buffalo gun the man carried, a Sharps. Although old, the gun looked to be in excellent condition. Fry was impressed by guns, and by the men who took good care of them.

He watched as the big man walked to the bar.

"What can I get you?" the bartender asked.

"A beer," Trapp said, setting the Sharps down and leaning it against the bar.

Trapp's eyes wandered to the bowl of hard-boiled eggs, and the sign.

"These eggs are free?" he asked.

The man set the beer down and said, "You get one with your drink."

"Much obliged," Trapp said, taking one.

He took out the five dollars they'd given him at the prison and set it on the bar. The bartender took it and made change.

"You just out?" the bartender asked.

Trapp took a moment to savor the first sip of beer as it went down and then said, "Why do you ask?"

"Oh, it's just that we get a lot of prisoners in here when they're released, and they usually pay with five dollars and look about as pale as you."

"I ain't a prisoner anymore."

"No," the bartender said, "of course you ain't."

Trapp picked up one of the eggs and hefted it.

"How do you eat this thing?"

"Ain't you ever seen a hard-boiled egg before?"

"No."

The only eggs Trapp had ever had were broken and mixed up. "Scrambled" somebody at rendezvous had once called them. There weren't many chickens in the mountains and the meals he usually had were either game meat or wild vegetables.

"You peel it," the bartender said.

Trapp frowned and said, "How?"

One of the saloon girls had been standing at the bar to Trapp's right a ways, and had heard the conversation. She moved closer to Trapp and he looked at her. She was the first woman he'd seen in twenty-five years.

She had dark hair, and a smooth complexion beneath her makeup. The scent of her tickled his nose and he started to feel somewhat foolish in her presence—especially since she'd heard him talking about the egg.

"Can I help you?" she asked.

"Well—" he said.

"Watch," she said. She took the egg and rolled it on the bar a few times, then held it up to show him that the shell was cracked. After that she started to peel it for him, until the shell was completely removed.

She held it out to him and said, "Now you can eat it like this or put salt on it."

"Thank you," he said, taking it.

"Don't mention it," she said, giving him a dazzling smile. He couldn't guess her age. He was well out of practice for that, and anyway the makeup was making it harder. He knew that she was a helluva lot younger than he was.

Hell, everybody was.

It was funny how inside he felt the same as ever, the same as when he'd been in the mountains. In prison, age didn't matter all that much either. This was the first time he fully realized that he was an *old man*. This pretty gal was helping him not because she was attracted to him, but because he was *old*.

He took a bite of the egg and chewed thoughtfully. The white tasted okay, but the yellow was too dry for him. He washed it down with a swallow of beer.

He turned his head to look around the saloon. It wasn't large, and all the tables had somebody sitting at them. He saw the woman walking around the room, talking to the men, smiling at them, and there were two other women as well. Looking at the three of them, he was able to see that the pretty woman who had spoken to him was the oldest of the three, although she wasn't the prettiest.

He bit the egg again and sipped the beer. He was nursing both because he didn't want to go through his money too fast. He hadn't yet decided whether he would buy some new clothes, or some black powder for the Sharps. Connors had given him some, but he needed more. There was also the problem of where to sleep. He'd gotten used to sleeping on a cot in prison. He didn't know now if he would prefer to sleep outside, or get a hotel room.

He didn't think he'd ever *been* in a hotel room before.

Suddenly, he thought of the wealthy father of one of the two men he'd killed. The man had not been able to get him executed, but he'd done the next best thing. He'd had Trapp sent to a prison far away from his beloved mountains, so that he wouldn't even be able to see them from a cell window.

For a long time, Trapp thought he would surely die in prison.

For some of the time he was there, he *wanted* very badly to die.

After a while that all faded away, along with White Dove's face, and the faces of the men he'd killed for killing *her*.

The funny thing was, he could still see the father's face, although he'd seen the man in court only once or twice.

He used to plan how he would gain revenge against the man when he got out, but now that he *was* out, he realized that the man must have been dead a long time. Twenty-five years ago he was as old as Trapp was now.

So now that he was out, there was not even revenge to look forward to.

All he had to look forward to was getting back to his mountains. To do that, he needed money to outfit himself for the trip.

He posed a question to himself.

How does a sixty-four-year-old man make money?

TWO

Fry was not the only one to notice Trapp when he entered.

Wes Gardner and Bob Stanley sat together at a table, watching the big man at the bar.

"He just got out," Gardner said.

"That means he's got five dollars in his pocket," Stanley said.

"Minus what he paid for that beer."

Stanley looked at Gardner and said, "We'd better get to him before he drinks up the rest of our money."

Gardner and Stanley lived in Littlesworth for a reason. One of the ways they made their money was to roll the cons who came out of Huntsville for the five dollars they were given. There were other, larger towns in the area, but Littlesworth had no real law.

"He don't look like much," Stanley said. "Why don't we just scare it out of him?"

Gardner grinned and both men stood up. They were both in their thirties, Gardner tall and rangy, Stanley shorter and stocky. The tall ex-con at the bar looked frail and old to them, one of the easier targets in recent months.

They walked to the bar and took up a position on either side of him.

Fry saw the two men rise and stand to either side of the old ex-con. They looked like a couple of vultures circling in for the kill. They must have known what Fry knew, that the man had just gotten out of prison.

What could they want from him?

What could they think he had?

Trapp felt the men on either side of him.

"Just get out, old man?" the man on his left asked.

Trapp turned his head slightly to look at Wes Gardner, and then to his right to eye Bob Stanley.

"Yep."

"Bet that beer tastes right good," the man on his right said.

"Good enough."

"Old fella like yourself, though," Gardner said, "shouldn't have more than one of those. Not when you just got out of jail. You're not used to that stuff."

Trapp stared straight ahead and said, "Make your point."

"We want to help you," Gardner said.

"Yeah," Stanley said, "we'll just take the rest of that five dollars off of you so you won't be tempted to have another."

"All right," Trapp said, "you've said your piece. Now move on."

Gardner and Stanley exchanged a glance and they both decided that the old fella must have been hard of hearing. He just didn't know what they were saying.

"Look, old timer," Wes Gardner said, "hand over the money and you won't get hurt."

Trapp looked Gardner—the man on his left—in the eye and said, "Move on, friend, or you will."

Gardner's eyebrows went up in surprise and he looked past Trapp at Stanley.

"Look, Grandpa—" Stanley said.

For some reason the word "Grandpa" ticked Trapp off. In prison everyone did the same work, and was the same age. Now that he was out, he wasn't about to start answering to "Grandpa," no matter how old he was.

He swung his elbow back so that it slammed into Stanley's gut, cutting him off in mid-sentence. As he did so, Gardner started to swing his fist and Trapp reached up and caught it in one of his huge hands. The years fell away from him as he squeezed. Wes Gardner's face screwed itself up in pain as the bones in his hand began to rub together. Trapp continued to squeeze until he had driven the man to his knees, and then released him. Gardner immediately cradled his hand to his body and began to rock back and forth.

Trapp turned to look at the other man, Stanley, and was in time to see the man straighten up and reach for his gun. He grabbed for the Sharps, but already knew that he would be too late. He was going to die

17

in a little saloon in a small town the very same day he got out of jail after twenty-five years.

As his hand closed over the barrel of the Sharps, he heard a shot. He felt no impact and looked in surprise at Bob Stanley, who had been driven against the bar by the force of a bullet, and now slumped to the floor.

He looked at the rest of the room and saw a man standing up by a table with his gun out.

"You looked like you could use a little help," the man said, holstering his gun.

"More than a little," Trapp said. "Thanks."

"Behind you!" a woman shouted.

Trapp turned and saw that Gardner, the man on his knees, was trying to draw his gun left-handed. He swung the Sharps back and caught the man on the butt of the jaw with the butt of his rifle. Something cracked, and Gardner slumped to the floor, unconscious or dead.

Trapp turned around and saw the woman who had shouted. She was the same one who had helped him with the hard-boiled egg.

"Thank you, too," Trapp said.

"Don't mention it," she said, folding her arms beneath her firm breasts.

The man who had shot Bob Stanley came over and checked the man over.

"He's dead," he announced, straightening up.

Trapp leaned over the other man and examined him. Apparently, the meeting of the butt-of-the-jaw with the butt-of-the-Sharps had resulted in a broken neck.

"This one, too," Trapp said. He looked at the woman and said, "You live here. What kind of trouble are we in?"

"Not much," she said. "These two, Gardner and Stanley, are no great loss and I'm witness that they started the trouble."

"What about the law?" Fry asked.

"What law?" she asked. "We got a sort of unofficial sheriff, but I wouldn't worry about him."

The bartender spoke up then.

"Somebody go and get Ben! This mess has to be cleaned up."

"Ben?" Fry said to the woman.

"Ben Frost. He's our unofficial sheriff."

"What's an unofficial sheriff do?" Fry asked.

"Cleans up," she said. She looked at Trapp and said, "You handle yourself pretty good for . . ."

"For an old man?" Trapp finished for her.

"I didn't mean—"

"That's all right, ma'am," Trapp said. "I appreciate your help here."

"My name is Annie," the woman said. "Annie Bennett." She extended her hand and Trapp took it after a moment's hesitation.

"John Henry Trapp, ma'am," he said, awkwardly.

"Glad to meet you, John Henry."

"Uh, if anyone cares," Fry said, "my name is Fry."

"Mr. Fry," Annie said, shaking hands with the younger man.

"I'm indebted to you, Mr. Fry," Trapp said, extending his hand.

Fry looked at the big hand and said, "If you don't mind, I've seen what you can do with that hand."

Trapp frowned, then withdrew the hand and grinned.

"Never to my friends," he said.

"While we're waiting for Ben to come over and make noises," Annie said, "why don't I buy the both of you a drink?"

"Sounds good to me," Fry said.

"I *would* like another beer," Trapp said.

Annie took hold of his arm and turned him back toward the bar. For a moment he felt one of her firm breasts pressed firmly against his arm.

Suddenly, he didn't feel sixty-four at all.

THREE

Ben Frost had an exaggerated idea of his own importance.

Frost, a man in his early thirties, had become the unofficial lawman of Littlesworth by default. After the elected sheriff had been killed two years earlier, no one else wanted the job. People in trouble began to go to Frost, because he knew how to handle trouble. Over the past two years he had "kept the peace" without benefit of a badge. What that amounted to was breaking up fights, jailing drunks, shooting wild dogs, and having the scene cleaned up after a serious altercation—like the one that had just taken place in the Lucky Star Saloon.

When Frost walked into the saloon, he did so with a flourish. He paused just inside the doorway for as long as it took the bat-wing doors behind him to stop swinging. He felt that this was ample time for everyone in the place to look at him.

21

"What happened here, Ed?" he said, speaking to the bartender.

He hadn't bothered to look down at the two bodies.

The bartender came out from behind the bar and approached Frost, explaining to him what had happened.

"Is he telling it like it happened?" Fry asked Annie Bennett.

"I'd say so," she answered. "Ed's a pain in the neck, but he wouldn't have any reason to lie."

While Ed was talking to Ben Frost, Fry helped himself to another hard-boiled egg and put a second in the other pocket of his vest. Trapp had decided that he didn't like hard-boiled eggs, and settled for working on the second beer. He wanted the excitement to be over so he could go and find a hole he could sit in and continue to plan his future.

"What are you doing to do?" Annie asked.

"Do?" Trapp asked.

"After this is all over."

"I . . . I'm not sure," Trapp said.

"Well, let's discuss the immediate future," Annie said. "Do you have a place to stay?"

"A place to stay?" Trapp repeated. He looked past Annie at Fry and the younger man simply shrugged his shoulders.

"Yes, a place to sleep? I mean, you did just get out of prison today, didn't you?"

"Yes, I did."

"So you'll need a place to sleep. I mean, you don't have much money, right?"

"No, not much."

"Then you do need someplace to sleep."

"I . . . yes, I do."

"All right," she said, smiling. She put her hand on his arm and said, "Come back after we close and meet me. All right?"

Trapp looked at Fry again, who nodded this time.

"A—all right."

"I'll talk to Ben."

She pushed away from the bar and went over to where the bartender was talking with Ben Frost.

Fry moved closer to Trapp.

"I wish she had made me that offer."

"What offer?" Trapp asked.

"She's giving herself to you, man."

"Giving herself?"

"Wake up, John Henry Trapp," Fry said. "She's gonna share her bed with you tonight."

Trapp stared at Fry for a moment, then looked at himself in the mirror behind the bar.

He looked at Fry again and said, "Why?"

Fry smiled, shrugged, and said, "I guess she likes older men."

Trapp looked into the mirror again and touched his face.

"I need a shave."

Fry slapped him on the back and said, "Now you're thinking straight."

Fry looked at Frost, Ed, and Annie having their conversation and said, "You know, if this guy doesn't have a badge, we don't have to talk to him."

Trapp looked at Fry and said, "You're right."

The conversation at the door ended. Ed the bartender hurried around behind the bar and Ben Frost walked very slowly over to where Trapp and Fry stood. The two bodies were still on the floor, where they'd fallen.

Frost looked around the room and said, "Tanner, get some boys and drag these poor bastards out of here."

"Sure, Ben," one of the men said. He got up and left the saloon.

Frost looked at Trapp and Fry.

"I believe I have all the pertinent facts in this case," Frost said officiously.

"What case?" Fry asked. "These two clowns tried to rob Trapp, here, and then tried to kill him."

"I have that information."

"Well, good," Fry said. "What else can we do for you, then?"

"I just wanted to tell your friend here," Frost said, "Trapp, is it?"

"That's right."

"I know a lot of fellas come out of prison with a grudge against the world, but—"

"I don't have any grudge," Trapp said.

"How long were you in?" Frost asked.

Trapp lifted the beer mug and took a drink.

"Look," Frost said, "I'm the law—"

"Show me your badge," Fry said.

"Hey—" Frost said.

"Show *me* your badge," Trapp said.

Frost looked at them both and then said irritably, "I don't have a badge."

"Then stop wasting our time," Trapp said. "Just clean up the mess."

Frost opened his mouth to speak but couldn't think

of anything to say. The fact that Trapp had spoken in a low voice and no one else in the saloon had heard him made it easier for Frost to back down.

"Why don't we finish these at a table," Fry suggested.

"Sure," Trapp said. He picked up his beer and his Sharps and followed Fry back to his table.

"Too bad you had to be bothered with this your first day out," Fry said.

"It wasn't too bad," Trapp said. "It could have been worse, if not for you."

"I just happen to like fair fights."

"What did you say your name was?"

"Fry," Fry said.

"Just Fry?"

"I don't much like my first name," Fry said, "so I don't use it."

"Oh."

"Where are you from, John Henry?"

"The mountains," Trapp said. "The Rockies."

Fry's eyebrows went up and he said, "A mountain man?"

Trapp nodded and said, "I guess."

"Well," Fry said, sitting back and looking at Trapp through new eyes, "a real mountain man. What the hell did you do to get put into Huntsville Prison, so far from the mountains?"

Trapp put his beer down and stared across at Fry.

"You saved my life," Trapp said, "so I'll tell you what I wouldn't tell that make-believe lawman. I was in Huntsville Prison because I killed two men twenty-five years ago."

Fry whistled.

"Twenty-five years in Huntsville?"

Trapp nodded, and then told Fry the story, of White Dove, the men who killed her, the father of one of the killers and his influence, and his twenty-five years in prison. . . .

FOUR

1846

John Henry Trapp was a patient man.

He knew that as long as he stayed on the trail of the men who had killed White Dove and burned his home to the ground, he would find them. He was especially confident because they did not appear to be running. It was very probable that they did not even know that they were being hunted.

Two weeks after he'd begun his hunt, he rode into the settlement called Pike's Landing. It was mostly tents and shacks, but it boasted a trading post that served liquor and beer. It also boasted a whorehouse with three women available.

Trapp dismounted and began to examine all the horses outside the trading post. One of the horses he was tracking had a chip in a shoe, which left a very distinctive track.

He tried the mounts in front of the trading post first, then moved over to the tent that housed the whores. There were three horses out front and he patiently lifted their hind hooves for his inspection.

The third horse had the chip in the shoe.

"Hey, there!"

Trapp turned and looked at the man who had called out and was now approaching. The man looked vaguely familiar to him. He was tall and slender, with an angular face that made it hard to guess his age, which was thirty.

"Can I help you?" the man asked.

"Is this your horse?" he asked, pointing to the animal with the offending horseshoe.

"No, it's not, but—"

"Then you can't help me."

The man frowned a moment and then said, "Don't I know you?"

Trapp studied the man for a moment before recognizing him.

"Is your name Pardee?" Trapp asked.

"That's right," Pardee said, "Nathan Pardee. You're John Trapp, aren't you?"

"I am."

"We met at the last Green River rendezvous."

"That was a few years ago."

"Yes, it was. What brings you here?"

"I'm hunting."

"Not much buffalo around here."

"I'm not hunting buffalo," Trapp said.

"Not much beaver, either—"

"I said hunting, not trapping."

Pardee frowned.

"Trapp—"

"Do you know who owns this horse?"

"I do," Pardee said.

"Who?"

"You're not hunting the owner of this horse, are you?"

"I am."

"No, Trapp," Pardee said, "let me tell you something. The man who owns this horse is connected with the Great Missouri Fur Company. Do you know who owns that company?"

"No."

"Sam Train."

"So?"

"You've never heard of Sam Train?"

"Can't say I have. Who is he?"

"A rich man," Pardee said, "a very rich man. He owns things, Trapp, and he owns people—important people."

"And he owns this horse?" Trapp asked, tossing a thumb at the animal.

"No, no," Pardee said, "his *son* owns this horse."

"His son?"

"Dan Train."

"He's riding with someone."

"Yeah, Toady Mcfarren, a real bad one. I don't know what your beef is, Trapp—"

"They killed my squaw and burned my home," Trapp said. "What would you do?"

Pardee let some air out of his mouth noisily and said, "I don't know, Trapp. I'm sorry, but I feel I've got to warn you—"

"You already have," Trapp said, cutting him off. "I thank you for that. Are they inside?"

"As far as I know."

Trapp nodded and turned to approach the tent. At that moment the flap was thrown open and a man and a woman appeared. The man was dressed, the woman was wearing something filmy that showed off large, overripe breasts. The man's arm was around her, his left hand cupping one of her breasts.

"That's Train," Pardee said, and moved out of the line of fire.

Train came out of the tent with the woman and was followed by a second man, who had to be Toady Mcfarren. Trapp could see how the man got his name. He was huge, and had a face like a toad. There was no woman with him. Trapp took notice of the fact that Mcfarren had two Kentucky pistols tucked into his belt. Trapp had a similar pistol in his belt, and was carrying his Sharps. Because of the woman, Trapp couldn't be sure what Train was carrying.

When Dan Train looked up from the woman's breasts, he saw John Henry Trapp standing by his horse.

"This your horse?" Trapp asked.

Train took his arm from the woman's waist and she backed away, bumping into Toady Mcfarren before slipping back into the tent.

"It is," Train said. "What's it to you?"

Train appeared to be about twenty-two, and having heard who his father was, Trapp was sure the young man had more than his fair share of arrogance. Behind him the man called Toady moved to his left, so that he was no longer directly behind Train. Toady was so ugly it was hard to guess his age, but Trapp was willing to bet on late thirties.

With the woman gone, Trapp could see the ornate, silver-encrusted handle of Train's Kentucky pistol.

"You've got a chipped shoe."

"Is that right?"

"Yes," Trapp said. "It led me right to you."

Train frowned.

"You've been looking for me?"

"That's right," Trapp said. "For two weeks."

"Whoa!" Train said, smiling. "You must want to see me real bad."

"I do," Trapp said. "You have no idea how bad— but I'm about to tell you."

"Go ahead, friend," Train said. "Whatever you want, I can afford it."

"Two weeks back you burned down a hut and killed a squaw. You probably raped her, too. Remember?"

Train frowned. White Dove was probably of so little consequence to him that he *was* having trouble remembering her.

Toady knew, though.

"Danny!" he shouted, immediately going for his pistol. He had it out of his belt when Trapp raised the Sharps and fired. The ball struck Toady right in the center of his ugly face, obliterating his nose, driving

31

through and taking out the back of his head. A woman chose that unfortunate moment to move the flap aside to see what was happening, and she was splattered with blood and brain matter for her trouble. She screamed and withdrew.

Train turned to look back just as Toady was falling. The man toppled forward and Train had to move aside to avoid being hit.

The young man stared at Trapp in horror and said, "You killed him!"

"That I did, son," Trapp said, "and you're next."

"Wait, wait—" Train shouted, his eyes wild, tears streaming down his face.

"Take out your pistol," Trapp said.

"No, no," Train gasped, "you'll kill me."

"I'm gonna kill you anyway, scum!" Trapp shouted. "Take it out!"

"Why are you doing this?" Train shouted desperately. "It was just a squaw."

"Maybe," Trapp said, removing his pistol from his belt, "but she was *my* squaw."

"Jesus, no," Trapp said. "I have money, I can pay you—"

"Not enough," Trapp said, "not nearly enough."

"Who are you?"

"Trapp," John Henry Trapp said, "the man who killed you. Now take out your pistol and die like a man, or get on your knees and die like a coward. Your choice."

To his credit—and to Trapp's relief—the young man reacted angrily.

"Damn you!" he shouted, and drew his pistol.

Trapp waited until he had it cocked before he shot the young man in the chest. The ball drove him back a few steps and he fell through the flap into the tent, out of sight. From inside there were numerous screams, and three women came running out in several stages of dress—or undress.

Trapp turned as Pardee came running over.

"Trapp," he said, "you'd better mount up and start running."

"I ain't running," Trapp said. "I didn't do anything wrong."

Pardee shook his head and said, "Tell that to Sam Train's money."

FIVE

1871

"And?" Fry asked.

"And I went to jail for twenty-five years," Trapp said.

"Sam Train's money?" Fry said.

"His money, and his influence," Trapp said.

"But he didn't have enough of either to get you sentenced to death."

Trapped swirled the last of the beer at the bottom of his mug and said, "Maybe he should have."

"Why do you say that?"

Trapp shrugged.

"I don't know the first thing about this, Kid."

"About what?"

"About this world," Trapp said. "I've been inside for a long time, Fry. Things have come and gone and changed and I've stayed the same—except for one thing."

"What's that?"

"I've aged, and I don't know the first thing about being old."

"Well," Fry said, "you didn't look so old when you were handling those two yahoos. Did you feel old?"

"Well . . . no—"

"Then who says you have to *be* old if you don't want to be?"

"What do you mean?"

"I mean to hell with the fact that you're . . . how old are you?"

"Sixty-four."

"Sixty-four?" Fry said, surprised. "Hell, you don't look that old."

"Thanks," Trapp said wryly.

"You've got a perfect opportunity tonight to find out how old you really are."

Trapp frowned, then said, "Oh, you mean the woman, Annie—"

"If you go home with that woman tonight," Fry said, "and nothing happens, then you'll know how old you truly are."

"I don't know," Trapp said. "You don't think she was serious, do you?"

"Oh, I sure do," Fry said. "I saw the look on her face while you were handling those two."

"Maybe she just feels sorry for me—"

"Sure, and maybe you remind her of her father," Fry said. "It doesn't matter *why*, Trapp!"

Trapp looked around, found Annie, and watched her for a few moments. She seemed to feel that he was looking at her and she caught his eye and smiled. He felt a tingle below his belt.

"You're only as old as you feel," Trapp said.

"That's the way to think, Trapp," Fry said.

"Yeah," Trapp said, looking at the twenty-five-year-old man sitting across from him. He smiled and said, "What the hell could a young whippersnapper know about it?"

"Nothing," Fry said, "nothing at all."

"Where are you staying tonight?" Trapp asked Fry.

"I have no idea," Fry said. "I thought one of these nice young ladies would take me under their wing—and their covers."

"Do you have any money?"

"Not much," Fry said. "Enough for a room or a girl."

"Wait a minute—" Trapp said.

"What?"

"I don't have enough money to pay this woman, Annie—" Trapp began.

Fry shook his head and waved his hands.

"From the sound of her invitation, Trapp, I don't think you'll have to worry about that."

"No?"

"No."

"Well then here," Trapp said, taking out some of the money, "take some of it—"

"No, no," Fry said, pushing it away, "I don't need your money."

"Take it—"

"You need it," Fry said, "don't you?"

"I need more than this," Trapp said, "so don't worry about it."

"Where are you headed, Trapp?" Fry asked, leaving the money on the table. "I mean tomorrow, after you leave here. Where do you want to go?"

Trapp looked past Fry, but Fry knew that he wasn't looking at anything *behind* him, he was looking at something *beyond* him.

"I want to go back to my mountain, Kid," Trapp said. "Back where I belong."

"That's a long ride," Fry said. "You'll need to get outfitted."

"Don't I know it," Trapp said.

"We'll see what we can do about that starting to-morrow," Fry said.

"We?"

"Sure," Fry said. "I was in San Francisco once, and I heard that the Chinese feel that when you save someone's life you become responsible for it."

"And you saved mine?"

"Well," Fry said, "I helped out . . . but seriously, I don't have anyplace special to go. Why don't I just help you get back to your mountain?"

"Why?" Trapp asked.

"Why not?" Fry asked.

Trapp studied Fry for a few moments and then said, "You ever been to the mountains?"

"Not me," Fry said. "I'm a flatlands man."

"All right," Trapp said.

"All right what?"

"All right, you can come to my mountain."

SIX

When Trapp woke up the next morning, he wasn't sure where he was. It was the first time in twenty-five years that he had not awakened in a cell on a cot. Once he had resolved that he was *not* in a cell, and that he was in a real bed and not on a cot, he had to deal with the other thing.

There was someone in bed with him.

He rolled over and looked down at the naked young woman in bed with him—or rather, it was *he* who was in bed with *her*.

He looked under the sheet and saw that he, too, was naked. His first urge was to get out of bed quickly, but he checked that. He took a moment to think about what had happened last night, and it all came back to him. . . .

He had met Annie Bennett after the saloon closed and had followed her to her room, above the general store. When they entered, she closed the door and turned to him, discarding her wrap.

"I find you interesting," she said, "and attractive."

"I'm a lot older than you," he said.

"I know that," she said, "but I've had younger men. I've had men younger than me, and men older."

"Have you ever been with a man my age?"

"No," she said, "but I'd like to be with you."

"I just got out of jail."

"I know that, too," she said. "Men who get out of jail are usually looking for a woman before anything else."

"Young men," he said.

She shook her head and moved closer to him, toying with the buttons of his clothes.

"They could have given you better clothes."

He laughed and said, "A better horse, too. I, uh, need a bath."

"I have a bathtub," she told him, unbuttoning his shirt. . . .

By God, he thought now, they had taken a bath together and he had put his hands on her firm, *slippery* young flesh. She had put her hands on *him*, and to his delight—and *hers*—he had reacted.

They had moved to the bed and made love, and he had been able to satisfy her—he *thought* he had satisfied her—no, he *felt* that he had satisfied her.

In his younger days, whenever he'd had sex with a woman—before White Dove—he had never worried about satisfying his partner. Sex was something that came rarely in the mountains, and when it did, a man enjoyed it. He didn't worry about whether or not the woman was enjoying it.

When he and Annie had started to make love, he'd found that old attitude coming back. Once he'd realized that he *could* still have sex, he decided to enjoy it. It was Annie Bennett who had slowed him down and had shown him how sex could be when *both* participants were enjoying themselves.

They had made love not once but twice during the night. She had awakened him during the night and he had been *sure* that he wouldn't be able to do it again, but she had been equally sure that he could—and then proceeded to prove it.

He had never been with a woman like her before—but then, when could he have ever met a woman like her twenty-five years ago in the mountains?

She rolled over at this point and opened her eyes.

"Want to run?" he asked.

She smiled and said, "Was that your first reaction?"

"I didn't know where I was," he said, "and then I didn't *believe* where I was."

"Well, trust me," she said, "you're here."

She stretched, causing the sheet to fall away from her bare breasts. It was the first time he had seen them in daylight, and they were as beautiful as they had been the night before.

She reached a hand out to him and ran it over his torso, then down below.

"Oh, no—" he said.

"Oh, yes," she said. "You have the constitution of a horse, mountain man . . . and the resemblance," she continued, moving her hand beneath the sheet and between his legs, "does not stop there. . . ."

The night before, Trapp had agreed to meet Fry for breakfast.

"We'll figure out how to pay for it then," Fry had said. Trapp wasn't worried about that. He had enough money for a couple of breakfasts, but that was about all.

He met Fry in front of a small café that Annie had recommended to them.

"Well," Fry said, "you don't look any the worse for wear. How did it go?"

Trapp hesitated, then grinned and said, "Surprisingly well."

"Me, too," Fry said. "One of the gals you left behind succumbed to my charms and was even willing to waive her usual fee. I have money to buy my own breakfast."

"Well then, let's eat," Trapp said. "For the first time in years, I'm starved."

Fry patted him on the back and said, "Welcome back to the world."

Book Two
Trapp and the Kid

SEVEN

Over breakfast they discussed money—or their lack of it.

"I have an idea, if you're interested," Fry said.

"What is it?"

"Well, those two ne'er-do-wells that we, uh, got rid of yesterday might have some paper on them."

"Paper?"

"Posters."

"You mean they might be wanted?"

"And there could be a reward."

"How do we check on that?" Trapp asked. The possibility sounded interesting. He didn't need a *lot* of money to get outfitted for his trip back to his mountain.

"Well, we could check with that fella Frost, the unofficial sheriff," Fry said, "or we could send a telegram to the closest town that has a real sheriff."

"I don't really want to talk to Frost again," Trapp said. "The man's attitude just didn't impress me."

"I agree."

"What's the closest town?"

"Portsville," Fry said.

"Can you send a message from this town?"

"I'll check and see if they have a telegraph office," Fry said. "You wouldn't know much about the telegraph, would you." It was more a statement than a question.

"I heard something about it while I was in prison," Trapp said. "Usually, when a new prisoner comes in, the other convicts pry the news of the world out of him. Being in prison is actually very educational."

"I'll learn all I can outside of the prison walls, if that's all right with you."

"I insist on it."

"There's just one thing," Fry said.

"What?"

"When I send the telegram, I'd like to do it in your name."

"Why?"

"My name might be . . . recognized."

Trapp stared at Fry for a moment and then said, "As what?"

"Well . . . I have a little bit of a reputation in some places."

"As what?" Trapp asked again.

"You should know this if we're going to travel together."

"Know what?"

"Some people call me 'Kid Fry.'"

"Why?"

"I, uh, am pretty good with a gun."

"You mean . . . like Paul Fountain?"

Fry looked surprised and said, "You know Paul Fountain?"

"He served five years with me," Trapp said. "He got out about three years ago."

"Well," Fry said, impressed in spite of himself, "I don't have the kind of reputation that Fountain has—"

"Well," Trapp said, "you're still young. You have time. How many men have *you* killed?"

Fry frowned.

"I'm sorry," Trapp said, "I shouldn't have said that, but I didn't like Paul Fountain at all, and I don't like the idea that you might be like him—or want to be."

"What was he like?"

"He was, and probably still is, a vicious animal. *He's* the one who should have been in there for twenty-five years, not me."

Trapp's vehemence was such that Fry wondered how much it must have wounded him to be in prison with a man like Fountain, and watch him walk out after only five years.

"I'm not like him, Trapp," Fry said. "It's important to me that you believe that."

"Are you wanted by the law?"

"No."

"Then I don't see why we can't travel together."

"I have to warn you," Fry said, "I get tested sometimes—by one man, or more."

"I'll back you."

Fry's eyes went to Trapp's Sharps, which was leaning against the table.

"What?" Trapp said. "Is something wrong with my gun?"

"Well, it's a little old," Fry said. "Don't you own a handgun?"

"I used to own a Kentucky pistol," Trapp said. "I don't know what happened to it after I went to prison."

"Have you ever seen one of these?" Fry asked, taking his six-gun from his holster and laying it on the table.

"Only in prison," Trapp said, not touching the gun. "The guards wore them . . . and Fountain talked about them . . . all the time."

"Pick it up," Fry said.

"No, thanks," Trapp said. "I'll stick with my Sharps. It suits my needs."

"You're not in the mountains now, Trapp," Fry said, "and you're not in the 1840s anymore. Everyone is carrying one of these now, and half of the people who do are anxious to prove they can use them."

"Like you?"

Fry stared at Trapp for a few moments, then sighed, took the gun off the table, and slid it back into his holster.

"You told me about your past," he said to Trapp, "so it's only fair that I tell you about mine. . . ."

EIGHT

1865

Wendell Fry was born in New York City.

He was an orphan, living in homes until he ran away at sixteen and started living in the streets. By the time he was nineteen he had been a member of a street gang called the Blind Cats for three years.

The gang lived in the basement of a rundown building in the area called Five Points, and was constantly at war with other gangs. In the three years he'd been a member, however, he had not killed anyone. He knew of other gang members who had, but the opportunity had never presented itself to him.

He always kept himself ready, though. He practiced constantly with an old Walker Colt he had stolen from a man in a restaurant. He used to go out to a field every chance he got to practice firing, but inside the city he always practiced moves without actually loading the gun.

He got so he could hit what he was shooting at almost every time.

Practicing with the gun got him interested in reading about the Old West—newspaper articles, dime novels, whatever he could get his hands on, and he finally decided that he would leave New York and go west.

He stole enough money for his train tickets and went first to Chicago, and then from there to Denver. He got off the train with the Walker Colt stuck in his belt, and walked right into trouble.

He didn't have enough money for a hotel and was walking around looking for a place to stay when he bumped into someone on the street—a man, walking with two other men.

The man got upset and called him street trash.

"How dare you touch me, you street trash," the man had shouted.

All three men were wearing guns and they fanned out in front of him. His heart was pounding. He had read about such confrontations in the dime novels, but had never expected to become involved in one—not right off the damned train.

"Look, I'm sorry—" he started.

"Look, Cole," one of the other men said, "he's got a gun."

"What are you doing with a gun, street trash?" the man called Cole asked.

Fry looked down at the gun in his belt and said, "It's my gun."

"What's your name, trash?" Cole asked.

"Fry," Fry answered, "Wendell Fry."

"Wendell?" one of the other men asked in disbelief. "Wen-dell?"

"That's my name," Fry said, grudgingly.

"And that's your gun, street trash," Cole said. "Let's see you go for it."

"What?"

"Your gun, son," one of the others said. "Draw it."

"Why?"

"Because if you don't," Cole said, "I'll kill you where you stand."

"I don't understand—" Fry began, but he saw all three men reach for their firearms and grabbed for his own.

Fry brought his out and cocked the hammer and pulled the trigger as quickly as he could. When he was done firing, all three men lay on the ground, dead.

1871

"One of the men I killed was named Clay Cole," Fry said.

"You killed Clay Cole?" Trapp said.

"And two other men," Fry said. "You've heard of Clay Cole?"

Trapp nodded and said, "In prison. You hear of most every lawbreaker with a reputation in prison."

From what Trapp had heard in jail, Clay Cole had been considered extremely fast and deadly with a gun—and Fry had killed him *and* two others.

"Well, I haven't broken any laws that I know of,"

Fry said, "but a Denver newspaper came out the following day calling me 'Kid Fry,' and the name stuck. No matter where I went, it stuck."

"Why didn't you go back to New York?"

"It never occurred to me," Fry said. "I mean, I was young then, and I was flattered by all the attention I was getting. Hell, some storekeepers even gave me some free clothes, and one shop gave me a holster. *This* holster that I'm still wearing."

"What did you do?"

"I stayed in Denver for about two weeks after that, and then some yahoo with a gun wanted to try me. I couldn't get out of it."

"And you killed him, too?"

Fry nodded.

"I left Denver the next day, but that name and the reputation that goes with it has been following ever since."

They sat in silence for a moment, then Trapp said, "All right."

"All right, what?"

"You can send the telegram in my name."

"Thanks."

They finished their breakfast, called the waiter over, and each paid for his own.

"This is all I have left," Fry said, showing Trapp a dollar.

"I have two."

"We'd better send a short telegram," Fry said. "They charge by the word."

They got up and walked outside, but before they

stepped into the street to cross, Fry put his hand on Trapp's arm to stop him.

"What?" Trapp asked.

Fry hesitated a moment, then said, "Wendell."

During the telling of the story he had refrained from mentioning his first name. He had simply said that Cole and his two friends had made fun of it.

"What?"

"My name," Fry said, "my first name. That's it. Wendell."

"Wendell," Trapp repeated. "Well, that's not so bad, Wendell."

"Maybe not," Fry said, "but now that I've told you, will you do me a favor?"

"What's that?"

"Don't ever call me that."

NINE

Trapp and Fry went to the telegraph office, where Fry composed as brief a message as possible to the sheriff of Portsville, Texas. As an afterthought he added the two words *Immediate response*. He thought it would be worth the extra cost.

Trapp waited outside, and when Fry came out he asked, "All done?"

"Now all we have to do is wait for an answer."

"Wait where?" Trapp asked. "We don't have a hotel room—"

"I told the clerk that I'd check back every hour. Until then I guess we'll just have to find something to do."

"Like what?"

"Well," Fry said, "if we're going to travel together, why don't we each show the other what we can do."

"About what?"

Fry touched his gun and said, "With this. I want to

see how well you shoot, and show you how well I shoot."

Trapp started to look around and Fry said, "Let's get our horses and ride outside of town—but let's stop at the saloon first."

"What for?"

"Empty whiskey bottles."

After they had pounded on the saloon door and collected some empty bottles from the annoyed owner, they walked to the livery stable. They each carried a sack with empty bottles, which clinked together noisily with every step.

Fry's horse was a handsome steeldust, and when Trapp saw it, he hesitated about pointing out the rundown mare he'd been given at the prison.

"Which one's yours?" Fry asked.

"Well," Trapp said, "you have to remember she's not really mine."

"All right."

"She was given to me when I got out."

"Okay."

"I wouldn't have—"

"Which one is it, Trapp!"

"That one," Trapp said, pointing.

Fry looked at the animal he was pointing at and made a face as if he'd stepped into a pile of horseshit— while barefoot!

"*That* one?"

"Yes."

"You actually rode that animal here?"

"I did."

Fry looked at Trapp and said, "I can see we're going to need more money than I thought. We've *got* to get you a new horse."

"How can we do that with no money?"

"Well, if those two yahoos were wanted, we'll have money."

"Waiting for us in Portsville."

"Right."

"But we still have to get there."

Fry looked at the horse again and then said, "Do you think she'd make it?"

"She got me here," Trapp pointed out.

"Let's see how she reacts to a short ride," Fry said. "Let's go shoot."

They saddled up, mounted up, then rode out of town. Once or twice Trapp had to shout at Fry to slow down, because he could feel his mount staggering as it tried to keep up.

"This is far enough," Fry said, dismounting.

Trapp got down and grounded the reins. He didn't think the animal had the energy to run off anyway.

They were standing among some low foliage and flat ground. Fry paced off twenty yards and set three whiskey bottles on the ground, then returned to stand next to Trapp.

"All right," he said, "I'll go first."

Before Trapp could reply, Fry drew and fired three times, shattering all three bottles in quick succession.

"I don't suppose that had anything to do with luck, did it?" Trapp asked.

"Nope," Fry said. He ejected the empty shells and reloaded, then returned the handgun to his holster.

"You can't do that with your Sharps," Fry said, folding his arms across his chest.

"Maybe not," Trapp said.

This time he picked up one bottle and paced off one hundred yards. He walked back to stand next to Fry, raised the Sharps, and fired. It was the first time he had fired the weapon—any weapon—in twenty-five years, but it was like falling off a log. The ball traveled straight and true and shattered the glass bottle.

"Your pistol couldn't have done that."

Fry squinted, then looked at Trapp and said, "I don't suppose *that* had anything to do with luck?"

"After twenty-five years?" Trapp said.

Fry squinted again then said, "Shit, I couldn't even *see* the bottle."

"I just caught a glint of sunlight off of it," Trapp said.

"Can you do that every time?"

"I could twenty-five years ago," Trapp said.

"Well," Fry said, "this demonstration is good enough for me. I'm willing to travel with you and have you back any play I make. I can promise you the same."

Trapp stuck out his hand and said, "That's good enough for me, Kid."

"Well, let's get back to town and see if we can't scare up some money."

When they got back to town, Trapp's mount was about to keel over. They handed their mounts over to the liveryman again, who demanded payment for the day. They dug into their meager finances and paid.

"Still think this one should be shot," the liveryman said, leading both horses into the stable. There was no doubt about which horse he was referring to.

"We're gonna have to get out of town by tomorrow morning," Fry said. "We can't afford to stay here one more day."

"If there's no reward, then what do we do?" Trapp asked.

"Let's not worry about that until the time comes," Fry said.

"Well, what do you usually do when you need money?" Trapp asked, persisting.

Fry hesitated before replying.

"I work," he finally said.

"Doing what?"

Fry stared at Trapp and let his hand come to rest on his gun in a very suggestive manner.

"Oh."

"I don't like to do it, Trapp," Fry said, "and I don't unless I have to. It's all I have to offer anyone in the way of talent."

"I understand."

Trapp had very little in the way of talent himself to be able to criticize young Fry.

They took a turn around town, getting further acquainted, and then headed for the telegraph office. Once again Trapp waited outside, and Fry returned in a matter of seconds.

"We're in luck."

"We are?"

Fry nodded.

"It's not big money, mind you, but they were each wanted to the tune of one hundred dollars."

"That's two hundred dollars!" Trapp said, his eyes wide. "How can you say it's not a lot?"

Fry put his hand on Trapp's shoulder and said, "The dollar simply doesn't buy what it did twenty-five years ago, Trapp."

TEN

Trapp and Fry rode into Portsville in the late afternoon of the following day.

They were riding double on Fry's horse.

When they reached the livery, they dismounted and handed the horse over to the curious liveryman.

"My friend's horse died a few miles outside of town," Fry explained.

"What about his saddle?" the man asked.

"It wasn't much of a saddle," Trapp said.

"I got some real nice saddles for sale."

"Have you got any used ones?" Trapp asked.

"Sure, but—"

"I might be back later to take a look," Trapp said.

"How about a horse?"

"That, too."

"I'll be here."

As they walked away from the livery, Fry said, "Why a used saddle?"

"I don't need a brand-new one, Fry," Trapp said. "A used one will do. Besides, if what you said about money is true, we'll have to use it carefully."

"Good point," Fry said, "although . . ."

"Although what?"

"Well, there is *another* way to make money."

"How?"

"Well, there are times when I've made money playing poker," Fry said.

"Are you good?" Trapp asked.

"Well, more lucky than good," Fry said, then added, "Uh, when I'm lucky, that is."

"Well, if we come across a game," Trapp said, "maybe I should play."

"You played poker in the mountains?"

"Not in the mountains," Trapp said, "in prison— and I became pretty good at it."

"Are you lucky?"

"I'll tell you what the man who taught me how to play told me," Trapp said. "When you're good, you don't need luck."

They were walking down the main street when Trapp started to veer off toward a hotel. Fry put his hand on his elbow, stopping him.

"Let's go and talk to the sheriff first and get our money."

Before leaving Littlesworth they had gone to see Frost, the "unofficial" sheriff, and had him write a note verifying the fact that they had killed the two wanted men, Wes Gardner and Bob Stanley.

They found the sheriff's office and knocked before entering.

The man behind the desk wore a sheriff's star on his chest. He was about fifty years old, with gray hair and a gray mustache.

"Sheriff?"

"That's right," the man said. "Sheriff Fulton. What can I do for you?"

They had decided that Trapp would be the spokesman.

"I sent you a telegram, sheriff, about two men named Gardner and Stanley?"

"Oh, yes, the reward," Fulton said. "Do you have verification?"

"Right here."

He handed over the note from Frost.

"What's an 'unofficial' sheriff?" Fulton asked.

"The town doesn't have a real sheriff, so this fella is a sort of acting sheriff."

The sheriff frowned at the note, then said, "Well, I suppose it's all right. There's not that much money involved anyway."

"Two hundred dollars," Fry said.

"I know," the sheriff said, "but the dollar doesn't buy what it used to."

The sheriff sat down and filled out a chit for two hundred dollars.

"Here, take this to the bank," he said, handing it to Trapp. "They'll give you the money."

"Thanks, Sheriff."

"I hope you don't mind me saying so, but you're a very unlikely-looking bounty hunter."

"I'm not—"

"Let's go, Trapp," Fry said, interrupting him.

"Who are you?" Fulton asked.

"I'm his partner," Fry said. "Thanks very much, Sheriff."

Fry opened the door and ushered Trapp out of the office.

"What did you do that for?" Trapp asked. "Now he thinks we're bounty hunters."

"Let him," Fry said. "At least he won't be asking any questions about us."

"Like your name?"

"Right."

They went directly to the bank and Trapp received the money from the teller.

"Let's get a hotel room," Fry said after leaving the bank, "and you can give me my half there, and not out on the street."

"Good idea."

They got one room with two beds, and Trapp registered, keeping Fry's name out of the book.

Up in the hotel room Fry dropped his saddlebags on one of the beds and sat down. Trapp counted out a hundred dollars and handed it to him.

"The first thing we'll have to do is get you a horse," Fry said. "It won't be an expensive one, but it'll be better than that bag of bones you had before."

"Right."

"You go and get the horse and rig, and I'll get the supplies we'll need to travel."

"We can do that tomorrow, Fry."

"What's wrong with tonight?"

"What you said about poker before has me interested. Let's go over to a saloon and see if there's a game."

"Are you sure you can win?"

"If I start to lose, I can always quit. Besides, I'd like to play just once in a game outside of prison walls."

"All right," Fry said, "I can use a beer anyway."

They left the hotel and went directly across the street to the Iron Horse Saloon. It was after dinnertime, so the saloon was doing a brisk business.

"Two beers," Fry said to the bartender.

He and Trapp both looked the room over. It was larger than the saloon in Littlesworth had been. Consequently it had more tables, more games, and more women working the floor.

"This reminds me," Fry said.

"Of what?"

"Did you say good-bye to Annie?"

"No, I didn't," Trapp said.

"Well, it probably doesn't matter," Fry said. "As long as you both got what you wanted from each other."

Trapp didn't reply.

"Did you?"

"I suppose so," Trapp said. "She satisfied her curiosity."

"And you?"

Trapp shrugged.

"I didn't want anything from her to begin with, so I guess I'm satisfied with what I *did* get."

Fry raised his eyebrows and said, "I'd be satisfied with that, too."

The bartender brought their beers over and Fry drank half of his down quickly. Trapp settled for a few sips.

"I've gone too long without this," he explained to Fry. "I want every one I have to last."

They drank their beer and studied the room. There were two house-run poker games going on, but Trapp wanted no part of those.

"The man who taught me the game warned me about house-run games," Trapp said. "The odds are always on the house's side."

"Well, there's a game over there that's not house-run," Fry said.

There was a table toward the back with four people playing poker. They were playing with paper money, so the stakes were decent for Trapp and Fry's purposes.

"All we need to do is maybe double our money," Trapp said. "That game looks like just the place to do that. Shouldn't take more than a few hours to win it."

"Or lose what you've got."

"This is not a prison, Fry," Trapp reminded him. "I can get up and walk out any time I want to."

One of the men at the poker table looked up and saw Trapp approaching.

"Looks like we've reeled one in, boys," Dan Smith said to the other three men.

"It's about time," one of the other men said. "I'm getting tired of passing the same money back and forth over and over again."

"Let's hope he's got enough to make it worth our while," Smith, the leader of the four, said.

The four men moved from town to town with their "private" poker game, playing until a stranger came over and asked to join them. When that happened the four of them proceeded to clean the stranger out, then leave town before anyone could figure out their game.

Smith watched this old codger approach the table and felt that they could play him all week and he'd never be the wiser.

Fry leaned against the bar and said to the bartender, "Let me have another one."

"Sure thing."

The bartender brought the beer over and Fry asked, "What do you know about that poker game?"

"Which one?"

"That table toward the rear."

The bartender squinted and said, "I don't know nothing about it."

"You don't know those men?"

"Nope," the bartender said. "They all came in together about an hour ago and started playing cards."

"Together? They all know each other?"

"Far as I can tell, they ride together."

Fry thanked the bartender, and decided to keep a close eye on the poker game.

ELEVEN

"You fellas mind if I sit in?" Trapp asked.

"Sure, old timer," one of them said. "Pull up a chair."

Trapp knew that he would hear himself called that a lot, but he didn't think he'd ever get used to it. Inside, he was still thirty-nine.

He pulled a chair out and sat down.

"What are the stakes?"

"It's a small game," the same man said, "a dollar and two. Dealer's choice, no limits on the raises."

Trapp knew *that* turned a lot of small-stakes games into larger ones.

They played for an hour, usually either five-card stud or draw, and Trapp won a little bit.

"What's say we raise the limit a little?" one of the men asked. "I'm gettin' sort of bored."

There was a general nodding of heads at the table and Trapp said, "Why not?"

"Five and ten?"

"Sure," Trapp said, and the others nodded.

Fry moved closer, trying to see everyone's hands—not the cards they were holding, but their *hands*. He was no expert, but if there was any cheating going on, he couldn't spot it. Besides, Trapp was winning.

Over the course of the next hour Trapp doubled his money and Fry was beginning to wish that the older man would quit. Even though he couldn't see anything going on, he had a feeling that *something* was.

At one point Trapp rose and walked over to the bar, where Fry was standing.

"How are you doing?" Fry asked.

"I'm up," Trapp said.

"Ready to quit?"

"Not yet."

"I think you should know—"

"Not now," Trapp said, "I want to speak to the bartender."

Trapp moved down the bar, spoke briefly with the barkeep, then came away with a beer and went back to the table to play cards.

During the third hour a big hand started to develop.

They were playing draw poker, and right off the deal there were two raisers. One of the men, named Borden, opened, the man named Dan Smith raised, and Trapp raised. Borden saw the two raises, then Smith reraised Trapp, who called.

Fry moved closer still, trying to see what Trapp was

holding. He could see that Trapp was holding two pair, Kings high. He wasn't sure how strong such a hand was in the face of two other bettors.

"How many cards?" the dealer, a man named Coleman, asked.

"One," Borden said.

"Two," Dan Smith said.

"I'll play these," Trapp said, and Fry frowned. He felt that Trapp should have at least taken one card.

Fry did not see the smile that briefly touched Dan Smith's mouth.

"It's up to you, Borden," Coleman said.

"Well, why don't we raise things up a little?" Borden asked. "I bet twenty. Any objections?"

"Not from me," Dan Smith said. "You fellas?"

No one else complained, including Trapp.

"Well, in that case," Smith said, "I'll call the twenty and raise forty."

The man to his left, Styles, said, "I'm out."

"I call the sixty," Trapp said, "and raise forty."

The dealer, Coleman, dropped out.

"You fellas must have some hands," Borden said. "I call the eighty to me, and raise a hundred."

"Call the hundred, and raise a hundred," Smith said.

Trapp counted out the money he had on the table and he was short forty dollars to call.

He looked at Fry and called him over.

"Let me have your hundred."

Fry stared at him and said, "Are you sure?"

"Let me have it."

Robert J. Randisi

Fry wondered if he'd read Trapp's cards wrong. Maybe he had *three* Kings and not just two. That would give him a full house.

Fry took out his hundred and handed it to Trapp.

"I call the two hundred to me," he said, "and raise another sixty."

That tapped him out—*and* Fry.

Fry saw some sort of eye contact between Smith and Borden, and the man called Borden said, "Well, I guess I'm out. You fellas look strong."

Now he knew something was going on, and Trapp was caught right in the middle of it—with all their money.

"Well, old timer," Smith said, "that just leaves me and you."

"I guess so," Trapp said.

Smith looked down at his money, counting it, then picked it up.

"Call the sixty and raise another sixty."

"I don't have another sixty," Trapp said. "I have no money left."

"I can't help that," Smith said. "Call or fold."

By now a crowd had gathered around the table, and all eyes were on Trapp.

"All right," he said. He reached for his Sharps, which was leaning against the table.

"Easy," Smith said as Trapp swung the gun up.

"This here's a Sharps Old Reliable," he said, setting the big gun down on the table, "in mint condition. It will cover the bet."

Smith's eyes widened when he saw the gun. He was in his forties, but he looked as if he recognized the gun for what it was. He ran his hand over the barrel, and then a crafty glint came into his eye.

"It's an old gun," he said. "I don't know if it will cover the entire amount."

"It covers it," Trapp said.

"That's what you say."

Trapp looked at Fry.

"What have you got?"

"Are you sure about this?" Fry asked.

Trapp simply stared at Fry.

"All right," Trapp said. He unbuttoned his shirt and slipped out a small ivory-handled derringer. "This should make up the difference."

He put the two-shot weapon down on the table and there was a murmur of assent from the crowd. They knew that the bet was now well covered. Smith couldn't back out, not with the crowd on Trapp's side.

"All right," Smith said, "the bet's covered." He smiled and fanned his cards out on the table. "Four aces," he said, and the crowd caught their collective breath. "Sorry, old timer."

"Hold it," Trapp said as Smith reached for the pot. Trapp fanned his cards on the table as well and said, "Straight flush, to the King. All black."

The crowd caught their breath again.

"What?" Smith said, shocked. He looked at Coleman, his gaze accusing.

"I swear, I didn't—" Coleman started to say, but he stopped himself before he could admit to cheating.

The most shocked man in the room was Fry. He *knew* Trapp didn't have *anything* like that in his hand.

"The pot's mine, young fella," Trapp said. "Sorry. Game's over."

"Now wait a minute—" Smith said.

Trapp didn't pick the Sharps up, he just swiveled it around on the table so that the barrel was pointing at Smith.

"You got a problem, Mr. Smith?"

Smith looked from the barrel to Trapp and back to the barrel again.

"N—no, no problem," he said. He pushed his chair back viciously and barked at the others, "Let's go."

On the way out he grabbed Coleman by the scruff of the neck and the other man said, "But I swear, Dan, I never—"

Trapp picked up the derringer and handed it back to Fry. The crowd began to move away and Fry sat down next to Trapp.

"I saw your hand," Fry said. "You had Kings over, no better."

"That's what they dealt me," Trapp said, making a neat pile out of the money.

"You mean you *knew* you were being cheated?"

"From the moment I sat down and saw the first deal," Trapp said.

"But how?"

"I was taught to recognize a crooked deal, and a crooked game," he said.

"And you obviously learned that lesson well," Fry said, "but . . . how the hell did you get that straight flush?"

"When I talked to the bartender," Trapp said. "I told him that they were cheating, and I wanted to teach them a lesson. I asked for some cards from an identical deck, and slipped them in on the last hand."

"I never saw that."

"They didn't either," Trapp said. "Nobody was supposed to."

"But you had all spades," Fry said, pursuing it further. "What would have happened if one of the same cards had shown up in his hand?"

"Cheaters have a fondness for aces," Trapp said. "That's why I made the straight to the King."

"But if it had—"

"If it had," Trapp said, cutting him off, "you would have had to back me." He smiled and handed Fry a stack of money. "Here's your half."

Fry took the money and said, "There must be five hundred dollars here."

"Six hundred and ten," Trapp said.

"You know," Fry said, "you've got to tell me more about this fella who taught you how to play poker."

"That's a story for another time," Trapp said, standing up. "Come on, I'll buy you a drink and then I'm going to turn in. Tomorrow we head for my mountain."

TWELVE

After they had a beer together, Trapp announced once again that he was turning in.

"How about you?"

"Well," Fry said, "I've got money in my pocket and it really isn't that late, is it?"

"Maybe not for you," Trapp said. "Maybe it's time—at least for tonight—that I started to act my age."

Trapp looked at Fry, but Fry was looking past Trapp at one of the saloon girls, a young woman with an impressive bosom and a bee-stung mouth.

"I'll leave you to act yours," Trapp said, turning to leave.

He stepped through the bat-wing doors and stopped for a moment outside. It was dark and it took him a moment to acquire night vision. When he could see, he stepped into the street and started across to the hotel.

He heard the first shot and turned quickly, bringing the Sharps up into position. The flash from the second shot showed him where the shooter was, and he fired his Sharps immediately. The ball struck the shooter in the midsection and continued on through, punching a considerably larger exit hole.

There was another shot, which apparently came from a rooftop. It struck the ground inches from Trapp's left foot. Trapp turned and ran, looking for cover from which he could reload and return fire.

After the first shot, everyone in the saloon fell silent. With the sound of the second shot, Fry moved immediately, running outside. He saw Trapp standing in the street, and saw the dirt in front of Trapp kicked up by a bullet.

Trapp turned and ran and Fry pulled out his gun. He ran into the street, looking up at the rooftops. A second shot was fired at Trapp, and Fry fired at the muzzle flash. The man cried out. The gun hit the ground just a second before he did.

Trapp had reloaded and now saw Fry moving toward him.

"What's going on?" Fry demanded.

"I don't know," Trapp said. "All of a sudden I was being shot at. Luckily, they're lousy shots."

"Maybe that's because they're poker players, and not gunmen?" Fry suggested.

"That thought had occurred to me," Trapp said.

"Well," Fry said, "there was four, and now there are two."

"Maybe the other two aren't in on this," Trapp said.

"We can sit right here until some law shows up," Fry said, "or we can try to find out."

"What do you suggest?"

"Well, I've never liked depending on someone else to save my bacon."

"I thought this was my bacon we're trying to save," Trapp said.

"Let's just say we're both in the same frying pan, at the moment."

"Then let's get out," Trapp said. "You go left, I'll go right."

"Ready," Fry said.

"Now!"

They both moved, and as they did, several hurried shots were fired.

Trapp went down to one knee and fired his Sharps one more time. The ball struck home, and the firing from his side stopped.

Fry threw himself into the street, rolled over twice, and then fired, silencing the firing from his side.

Both men stood up just as a man wearing a badge ran up on them, followed by two other men. They all had their guns drawn.

"What the hell is going on here?" the sheriff demanded.

Trapp and Fry left the sheriff's office after having explained the evening's happenings to him. Their story was backed up by several witnesses from the saloon, including the bartender.

"All right," Sheriff Roy Macklin said, "I buy what you're selling me, but that doesn't mean I don't want the two of you out of my town by tomorrow morning."

"All we need is time to stock up on supplies," Trapp said, "and then we'll be gone."

As they started to leave, the fortyish sheriff called out, "Hey, friend."

They both turned.

"You," Macklin said, pointing his finger at Fry. "Don't I know you?"

"I don't think so," Fry said.

"What's your name?"

Before Fry could answer, Trapp said, "Trapp."

"No, not your name," Macklin said, "him."

"I told you his name," Trapp said. "Trapp."

The sheriff frowned.

"He's my son," Trapp said, and opened the door for Fry.

On the street Fry said, "Your son?"

"Do you want to go back in and tell him your real name?"

"No, Daddy."

"I'm gonna do what I set out to do," Trapp said. "Turn in."

"I'm going back to the saloon," Fry said. "I'll be in later."

"Don't come in too late, sonny," Trapp said.

"Yes, Poppa."

Trapp went to the hotel room, stripped to the waist, and lay down on the bed. He thought about the way he'd felt when he spread those cards on the table—knowing that *he* had slipped the entire hand into the game in plain sight of a saloon full of people.

He hadn't felt *that* alive in years—not even when he was having sex with Annie Bennett.

He thought back to the man who had taught him how to do that—and that made him think back to certain other parts of the past twenty-five years.

Book Three

Inside

THIRTEEN

Huntsville Prison, 1846

After the thirty-nine-year-old John Henry Trapp had gone through the ignominy of being shaved, shorn, bathed, and dressed, he was escorted to the warden's office before he was even shown to his cell.

The guard walked him into the warden's office and the man behind the desk stood up.

"All right, guard," the warden said. "You can go."

"Warden," the guard said, "he's a killer—"

"You can go," the warden said again.

The guard backed out and closed the door.

"Sit down, Mr. Trapp—or can I call you John?"

"Trapp."

"All right, Trapp," the warden said. "My name is Warden Bellows."

Trapp didn't respond, and he didn't sit.

"The reason you're here is because I want to warn you about a few things," Bellows said.

"Like what?"

"Well, basically I wanted to warn you that a fella your size is liable to run into some trouble right at the beginning of your term."

"You mean there's trouble in here?" Trapp said. "I would never have guessed."

"The cons in here are going to want to try you out right away," Bellows said.

"I can take care of myself."

"I'm sure you can," the warden said, "but I have to tell you that I wouldn't take very kindly to having you *kill* anyone while you're here."

"Is it all right if I break a few bones?" Trapp asked sarcastically.

"You can do anything you have to do to protect yourself and earn yourself some respect," Bellows said, "but I do not want you to kill anyone."

"I see," Trapp said. "Is that all?"

"Just so long as you know the rules."

"All of the rules were explained to me while they were dousing me with buckets of water."

"I mean my rules."

"Your rules," Trapp said. "Right, don't kill anyone."

"Right."

"I understand."

"Good," the warden said. "Guard!"

The guard came in quickly, as if he expected to find something wrong.

"You can take Mr. Trapp to his cell."

The guard looked from Trapp to Bellows, wondering if they were keeping something from him, then said to Trapp, "Come on."

Trapp went out into the hall. At that time he didn't know how soon the warden's warning would be put to the test.

Trapp was put into a cell with three other men, two bank robbers and a kidnapper.

"I didn't kidnap anyone," Jerry Heald said when he introduced himself to Trapp.

"Of course not," Sid Green said, "and Walter and I didn't rob any banks."

"Of course not," Walter Pierce said.

"What are you here for?" Green asked.

"For killing two men."

"But you didn't do it, right?" Green asked.

"Wrong," Trapp said. "I did it."

"Well, well," Green said, "somebody who's in here for something he *did* do."

Sid Green and Walter Pierce were both in their thirties. They had each been there for four years, with one more to go on their sentence.

Jerry Heald was in his late twenties. He'd been there for three years and had seven left on his sentence.

"I don't belong here," he complained. "I'll be an old man when I get out."

"I'm older now than you'll be when you get out," Trapp said, "and I'm here for twenty-five years."

"You can take some of that off for good behavior," Green said.

"No," Trapp said, "I can't."

He knew that the father of one of the men he killed

would use his influence to make sure that never happened. In fact, he wouldn't have been surprised if the man tried to have him killed while he was in here.

"You're a bad one, huh?" Green asked, misunderstanding.

"As long as I'm left alone," Trapp said, "I'll be fine."

"Well, somebody your size," Green said, "I doubt that will happen. They'll be trying you out as early as today, you can be sure of that."

"Who will?"

"The ones who run this place."

"The guards?"

"No, not the guards," Green said derisively. "They work here, but they don't run the place. I mean cons like Big Teddy Speck and his people, Billy Kirk and his crew. There are several different groups fighting for control in here."

"And which group are you a member of?" Trapp asked.

"Some of us stay outside the group and watch our step, Trapp," Green said. "You, on the other hand, because of your size, will first be tested, and then courted."

"Courted?"

"Sure," Green said, "all of the groups will want you on their side—especially when they find out what you're in here for."

"Like I said," Trapp said, "all I want is to be left alone."

"Well, *we'll* leave you alone," Green said, "but I can't say that others will."

Trapp sat down on an empty lower bunk and said, "That will do for a start."

The next day after breakfast the prisoners were allowed outside for a short time, an exercise period.

Trapp's three cellmates moved to one side of the yard, away from the others. Trapp wandered the yard alone. Studying the other prisoners, he could see what Green had been talking about. There were some people, like himself and his cellmates, who were off to themselves, but for the most part the prisoners gathered in groups, and in the center of the group was the leader, being kept safe from harm.

Trapp was watching one such group, because the man in the center interested him. He was not as tall as Trapp, but he *was* the biggest man Trapp had ever seen. He looked almost as wide as he was tall, and yet he was not fat.

He wondered if this was the "Big" Teddy Speck whom Sidney Green had mentioned.

He became aware of a movement behind him and turned just in time to avoid being stabbed in the back. He grabbed the man by the wrist and twisted. The weapon fell to the ground and he saw that it was a knife fashioned from a spoon.

The man, six feet and in good shape, glared at him and tried to pull his hand free.

"Hey, fella," the man said, "no hard feelings, huh? I was just doing a job."

"Sure," Trapp said, "no hard feelings."

Trapp slid his grip up the man's arm to the elbow,

then grasped the man's wrist with his other hand and promptly broke his forearm like a dried twig.

The man screamed and sank to the ground when Trapp released him. The man apparently had some friends, and two other men charged Trapp. The big man pivoted and lifted his foot, actually planting it into one man's face as he charged him. The man fell back, his nose squashed flat, his face covered with blood.

The third man threw a punch, which Trapp allowed to land. The blow had little effect as it struck his cheek, and then he hit the man. The blow snapped his head back and the man sank to the ground, unconscious.

By this time several guards had rushed forward, and two of them took hold of Trapp's arms. The big man did not resist.

"Take him to the warden," a third guard said. He turned to some prisoners and said, "Pick these men up and take them to the infirmary."

Trapp was escorted across the yard and he knew that he was the center of attention. As he walked past his cellmates, he saw Green smile and nod to him, as if telling him that he had done well.

He was standing in front of the warden's desk, waiting for the man to speak to him.

Finally, Bellows looked up from reading a report.

"You broke one man's arm, another's nose, and a third's jaw," he said.

Trapp smiled at the warden and said, "Satisfied? None of them are dead."

"No," the warden said, shaking his head, "nobody's dead—yet."

FOURTEEN

The next day he was approached by two men in the yard.

"Big Teddy wants to talk to you."

"Good," Trapp said, "I want to talk to him."

He followed the two men over to the group that surrounded Big Teddy.

"Let him through," Teddy Speck said.

Up close, Trapp could see that Teddy Speck was a few years younger than himself. He was surprised to find that the man was under six feet tall.

"Your name is Trapp?"

"That's right."

"You're in for murder, aren't you?"

"Right again."

"Did you do it?"

"I did," Trapp said, "and I'd do it again."

Teddy Speck smiled.

"I can use a man like you."

"I'm not interested."

"Don't be so hasty, Trapp," Speck said. "If you join me, there will be a lot of privileges."

"I'm only interested in one privilege."

"I have the power to grant it."

"All I want is to be left alone."

Speck stared at Trapp for a few moments, then said, "Have you had other offers already?"

"You're the first I've spoken to," Trapp said, "but I'll tell others the same as I've told you—leave me alone."

"That's not possible," Speck said. "You're too valuable to walk the fence like your cellmates. If you are not on my side, you are against me."

"I'm not your enemy."

"I could break your back now," Speck said. He straightened to his full height of possibly five-ten. With his bulk he was an imposing figure.

"If you had that much nerve," Trapp said, "you wouldn't be hiding behind all these men."

Teddy Speck surprised Trapp and smiled.

"You haven't been here long enough, Trapp. You don't know that I'm a target, just like Billy Kirk and a few others. We run this place. We say who is neutral and who isn't—and you, my friend, just don't qualify."

Trapp turned to walk away and found his path blocked. He waited, staring at the man standing directly in front of him.

"Let him go," Teddy Speck spoke finally. To Trapp he said, "Think about my offer, Trapp. I can get you anything—food, drink . . . women?"

Trapp turned and said, "Can you get me released?"

"If I could do that," Speck said, "would I still be here?"

"You heard the man," Trapp said to the men blocking his path. "Let me pass."

They opened a path for him and he used it.

"Think about it, Trapp," Speck called out. "Give me your answer tomorrow."

That afternoon Billy Kirk made his move.

"Come on, Trapp," a guard said, unlocking the door to Trapp's cell. "Somebody wants to see you."

"Who?" Trapp asked.

"You'll see."

The guard opened the door and Trapp walked out. He waited while the guard locked the door again and said, "This way. Walk ahead of me."

After they had gone a hundred yards or so, Trapp said, "This isn't the way to the warden's office."

"We're not going to see the warden."

"Then who?"

They reached another block of cells and there was one with the door wide open.

"In there," the guard said.

"I don't understand."

"The man who wants to see you is in there."

Trapp looked at the open door, then walked toward it. There was a convict standing on either side of it, but they made no move to stop him.

"Come in, Trapp," a voice said from inside.

Trapp entered and saw a man sitting in an overstuffed easy chair. The wall bunks had been folded up to give him more room. Obviously, he shared the cell with no one.

As Trapp entered, the man stood up. He was in his early forties, slim, dark-haired, and when he spoke, it was obvious that he was educated.

"I'm Billy Kirk."

Now Trapp understood. Kirk was about to make his offer, as Speck had made his.

"I saw what happened in the yard yesterday," Kirk said.

"Everyone did."

"I'd like you to work for me."

"I don't think so."

"You haven't heard my offer yet."

"I don't have to," Trapp said. "I bet it will sound just like Teddy Speck's offer."

"Ah, Teddy," Kirk said. "He got to you first, did he?"

"That's right."

"Then you're working for him?"

"No, I'm not."

Kirk looked happy.

"Then you're available to work for me."

"No, I'm not."

Kirk frowned.

"Who are you working for then. Simmons? Taylor? They can't offer you what Speck and I can."

"I'm working for myself, Kirk," Trapp said. "I want to be left alone."

"Look, Trapp, a man of your abilities—"

Trapp held up his hand to stop Kirk.

"I've heard this from Speck. You are both going to have to accept the fact that I want to be left alone. I don't want to work for either of you."

"We can't do that," Kirk said. "You're a potential weapon—"

"Only for myself," Trapp said. "I'm sorry, Kirk, but you and Speck will have to wage your struggle for control without me."

Trapp turned and the two men outside moved to block his path.

"Make them move," Trapp said.

"Think about it, Trapp," Kirk said. "You'll see that you have to make a choice, one way or another."

Trapp didn't answer. He saw one of the men watching Kirk behind him, and then the two men suddenly moved out of his way.

Trapp found the guard several cells away and said, "I'd like to go back to my cell now."

The guard looked at Trapp, surprised, then said, "This way, then."

On the way back to his cell, the guard asked Trapp, "So which one you gonna work for?"

"Neither."

"Was I you," the guard went on, as if he hadn't heard Trapp's reply, "I'd work for Big Teddy. He and Kirk are in here for a long time, but I think in the long run Big Teddy is gonna be in total charge soon."

"How soon?"

"A year, maybe two."

"That long?"

91

"Hey, it takes a while to gain control. Hell, they're in for another ten each, at least," the guard said. "How long are you in for?"

"Twenty-five."

The guard's eyes widened and after a moment he said, "Shit, by then you should own the place."

FIFTEEN

1851

Five years later Trapp was still being left alone, by Big Teddy and his people, by Billy Kirk and his people, by everyone—even the guards.

He went his own way, had his own routine. During the first four months he was in Huntsville he broke two jaws, four arms, and three legs.

Nobody was killed, and the warden was happy—relatively.

1857

Eleven years. Big Teddy and Billy Kirk were gone. Big Teddy finally caught it in the back with a spoon/knife by one of his own men. Billy Kirk was released. Nobody ever knew if Kirk had Big Teddy killed or not. It could have been anyone with the right price.

After Teddy and Kirk had left, their people floundered around for a while, looking for a new leader. Some of them even approached Trapp about being a leader, but he refused.

Over the first eleven years Trapp went through nine different cellmates. They had all been released, allowed to return to their worlds while he remained inside, away from his.

Trapp had accepted his fate early. He didn't sit in a corner pounding his head against a wall like some of the newcomers did. He didn't pick fights with the other convicts, testing death every day. He did fantasize about revenge, but that faded. The only man he could have revenge against would be dead by the time he got out.

He wondered how long after the man's death his influence would last. May he'd get out a year or two early, if the man died early enough.

And maybe not.

1861

Fifteen years.

Trapp had his beard and long hair back. Nobody bothered telling him to cut it anymore, not even the new young warden.

He didn't feel any older, although he knew he looked older than when he had first arrived. Age didn't mean anything inside. Everybody was the same age—inside it was *strength* that made the difference, and there was no one in Huntsville who wanted to match strength with Trapp.

He made no friends, not once in fifteen years. His cellmates were just that, people he shared a cell with, and they soon came to accept that. They did, however, benefit from that fact, because no one wanted to tangle with Trapp's cellmates. Even though they weren't his friends, it still wasn't known how he would take it.

For fifteen years Trapp got what he wanted.

He was left alone.

During the sixteenth year, John Welcome arrived at Huntsville.

Welcome was a notorious gambler and lady's man, and for a while the others wondered which of those avocations had gotten him to Huntsville.

Welcome didn't talk to anyone, not even his cellmates. He was a private man, maybe even more private than Trapp.

The gambler was in his early forties and the others eventually learned that he was serving seven to ten for killing a man over a woman—after he had cleaned the man out in a poker game.

Everyone in Huntsville was waiting for Trapp and Welcome to come face to face.

They managed to avoid each other for two years.

1864

The door to the warden's office opened and John Welcome stepped out.

"Trapp, isn't it?" he said.

"That's right."

"I'm John Welcome."

"I know."

"I understand you've been here a long time."

"That's right."

"I've been here two years, and I don't know anyone I can talk to."

"So?"

"So maybe we can talk."

"Why me?"

"Why not?"

They stared at each other for a few moments.

"Maybe," Trapp said, and stepped into the warden's office.

Warden Bill Blair had taken over three years ago. He was young, about thirty, when he took the job. His hair was always cut, he never looked as if he needed a shave, he always wore a tie, and he never went anywhere inside without at least four guards.

He was the wrong man in the wrong job.

"Sit down, Trapp."

"I'll stand."

Blair frowned.

"You pretty much go your own way, don't you, Trapp?"

"Yeah."

"Everyone in here respects you," Blair said. "The inmates, the guards . . . everyone."

"So?"

Blair set back in his chair and said, "I want you to be a trustee."

Trustees were convicts who were given certain privileges as long as they performed certain functions for the warden. The other convicts did not look kindly on trustees. They felt that they were spies.

"No thanks."

"I know that the inmates don't like trustees," Blair said, "but you and I could change that."

"How?"

"If you took the job, the others would think differently about trustees, simply because you were one," the warden explained. "What do you think?"

"I still think the same thing," Trapp said. "No thanks."

"Trapp—"

"I'd like to go back to my cell now."

Blair leaned forward and stared at Trapp.

"You're disappointing me, Trapp."

"You're ruining my day," Trapp said. "I'd like to go back to my cell."

Blair assumed what he must have thought was a menacing look, but to Trapp he just looked ridiculous.

"You think you own this place, Trapp," the warden said. "You're wrong."

"I don't own anything, Warden," Trapp said, "and I don't want to. All I've ever wanted is to be left alone."

"Well, you've been left alone, my friend, for fifteen years," Blair said, "but you've got another ten to do. Think about it."

Trapp didn't respond.

"Guard!" Blair yelled. When the guard came in, the warden said, "Take Mr. Trapp back to his cell."

"Yes, sir."

In the hall Trapp said, "Take me to John Welcome's cell."

"What?"

"The gambler, Welcome."

"Aw, come on, Trapp," the guard said, "I got to take you to your cell."

"You will," Trapp said, "after you take me to John Welcome's."

Welcome looked up as Trapp appeared in the doorway of his cell.

"You fellas want to excuse us?" he asked his cellmates.

"Sure," one of them said, and all three of them filed out past Trapp—gingerly.

Trapp stepped into the cell. Welcome sat on his bunk with a deck of cards.

"What can I do for you?" he asked.

"You said you wanted to talk."

Welcome stared at Trapp for a long moment, then said, "So sit down and talk."

Trapp hesitated and then sat.

"You ever play cards?" Welcome asked.

"Some."

"Poker?"

"Some."

"You any good?"

"No."

"Why not?"

Trapp shrugged.

"Not smart enough, I guess."

"Nah," Welcome said, "you're smart enough. Maybe

you don't concentrate enough." Welcome showed Trapp an ace, then passed a hand over it and seemed to change it to a King.

"How did you do that?"

"I concentrated," Welcome said, "and you didn't. Now, watch again."

Welcome did it again, and Trapp still didn't see a thing.

"You're still not concentrating," Welcome said. "I can teach you to concentrate, if you'll let me."

Trapp hesitated a moment, then shrugged and said, "Why not?"

"Watch," Welcome said.

"Before you start," Trapp said, "what did the warden want you for?"

"He asked me to become a trustee."

"Yeah, me too."

"What did you tell him?"

"I told him to forget it."

"Yeah, me too. Are you watching now?"

"Yeah, I'm watching."

"Well, *don't* watch . . . concentrate!"

SIXTEEN

1866

"You know," John Welcome said to Trapp, "for a man with hands the size of yours you really picked this up quickly."

"Quickly?" Trapp repeated. "It's been two years, John."

"I know," Welcome said, "but it took me four. You're a natural, and it's amazing with hams like that for hands."

"It wouldn't have taken so long if we'd been able to be cellmates," Trapp said.

"Ah, the warden would never allow that."

"Well, he may not be warden much longer," Trapp said.

"What have you heard?"

"Some of the guards say that he's being replaced soon," Trapp said.

"It couldn't happen to a nicer guy," Welcome said. "Come on, let me see you deal seconds again."

For the first time in years, Trapp had a man he could call his friend. It was an odd alliance, an educated gambler and a man from the mountains, and the other convicts wondered about it.

From the point of view of Trapp and Welcome, it was simple. They were each the only person the other had met who didn't claim he was innocent.

Trapp freely admitted that he'd killed two men with good reason, and would do it again.

Welcome's contention was that he killed in self-defense, saving not only his own life but the life of the woman involved as well.

They were the only ones who weren't constantly trying to find someone who would believe they were innocent.

Trapp dealt out a hand of five-card draw, deliberately giving Welcome three aces and himself nothing. Welcome drew two cards, and he drew three. Welcome did not improve, and Trapp introduced some foreign cards into his hand and ended up with a straight flush to the King.

"That was excellent," Welcome said, his tone admiring, "truly excellent."

"Did you see it?"

"Well, of course I saw it," Welcome said. "Any professional gambler would have seen it, but it was still excellent. I just wouldn't try it on any professionals for a while."

"Hell," Trapp said, "I probably won't have any use for this skill at all, ever."

"You never know, Trapp," Welcome said wisely. "You just never can tell."

1871

"Well," John Welcome said.

"Yeah," Trapp replied, "well."

"I guess it never dawned on us that you'd be getting out before I did," Welcome said.

"I never thought you'd serve your full sentence," Trapp said, looking around his cell.

"And you?"

He looked at Welcome.

"Hell, I always knew I'd serve mine out," Trapp said. He was still looking around.

"What are you looking for?" the gambler asked him.

"I don't know," Trapp said, looking bewildered. "I honestly don't know. It just seems that after twenty-five years there should be something that I'd want to take with me."

"Here."

"What's this?"

Welcome handed Trapp a well-used deck of cards.

"Take that with you, to remember me by."

Trapp took the cards, looked at them for a moment, and then tucked them into his shirt pocket.

"Well," he said, "I'm all packed."

"Better get going before they change their mind," Welcome said.

Trapp started toward the open cell door then stopped.

"What is it?" Welcome asked.

"I don't know," Trapp said. "I just got this feeling . . . that I don't know who I am, or where I'm going."

"You're Trapp," Welcome said, "and you're going to your mountain." Welcome moved next to him and put his hand on the bigger man's shoulder. "Don't ever let anyone get between you and it, Trapp . . . not anyone!"

"What are you gonna do when you get out in a year?" Trapp asked.

"I don't know," Welcome said. "I haven't been inside as long as you. Things won't have changed as much."

"I know," Trapp said. "It's not the world I left out there."

"No, it's not," Welcome said. He squeezed his friend's shoulder hard and spoke urgently, hoarsely. "Just go to your mountain, Trapp. From what you've told me, it won't have changed."

"I hope not," Trapp said. "That's what I'm holding on to, John. If it's changed . . ."

John Welcome heard something in John Trapp's voice that he had never heard before. He wasn't sure, but it might have been . . . fear?

"If it's changed," Welcome said, "you'll find something else to hold on to."

Trapp didn't reply for a moment and then he said, "What about you?"

"Me?" Welcome said. "I hold on to a deck of cards. Cards don't change, Trapp—like mountains."

Trapp found himself fervently hoping that John Welcome was right—on both counts.

* * *

Trapp came back to the present, sitting up in his bed. He went to the window and opened it, letting in the cool air. He could hear the voices and music from the saloon across the street.

What would he do, he wondered, if somehow the mountains had changed?

What would he hold on to then?

SEVENTEEN

The next morning Trapp and Fry had breakfast and then went looking for a horse.

"We've got enough money now to get you a decent horse," Fry said.

"That's all I need," Trapp said, "a decent mount to get me to the mountains."

"You know," Fry said as they continued to walk toward the livery, "with the money we've—the money *you* won—we could get ourselves a couple of real nice ponies—mustangs, maybe."

"You can spend a lot of your money on a horse if you want to," Trapp said. "I'll just take a decent, competent animal and save my money for something else."

"Like what?"

"I don't know," Trapp said, "but I feel a little better about being out of prison and in a strange world now that I have some money in my pocket."

"That's called security."

"I guess so," Trapp said. "Don't you want a little security in your life?"

"I don't know," Fry said. "I think I'm a little young for that—if you don't mind my saying so."

"Go ahead and say it."

"I'm just afraid I'll lose my edge."

"Your edge?"

"Yeah, you know, I'll relax too much and some young buck—*younger* buck—will come along and put me down. When you're a walking target, Trapp, you've got to keep alert at all times."

"Stay in the mountains with me," Trapp said. "You can't get into trouble there."

Fry gave Trapp a surprised look and said, "Look who's talking."

Trapp opened his mouth to reply, then realized he had nothing to say to that. Fry was absolutely right.

"End of advice," he said as they reached the livery.

They went out back with the liveryman, who showed them some expensive horses. Trapp finally picked out an aged gelding who looked as if he still had some good miles in him and bartered the man down to fifty dollars. He also gave him five dollars for one of the used saddles he had.

"You drive a hard bargain," the liveryman said, counting his money.

"Sure," Trapp said, saddling his animal.

"What about you, young fella?" the liveryman asked Fry. "You looking for a new horse?"

Fry eyed a healthy-looking young mustang that the

man had in his corral, but then shook his head and said, "No, the animal I've got is good enough."

"You sure?"

"I'm sure," Fry said.

"Suit yourself," the man said, then tried another tack. "You fellas traveling far? I can offer you a good deal on a pack animal."

"No thanks," Trapp said. "We'll travel light."

Fry proceeded to saddle his horse and then he and Trapp rode to the general store.

"Why travel light?" Fry asked when they reached there. "With a pack horse we wouldn't have to stop along the way for more supplies."

"I would just feel slowed down by a pack animal," Trapp said. "If we use our supplies sparingly, we'll get where we're going a lot faster, even with a few stops for more supplies."

Fry shrugged and said, "It's your trip, you call the shots."

They went inside and bought enough supplies to split evenly between them so that they'd each be carrying a fair-sized sack tied to their saddles.

Outside, as they mounted up, Fry said, "Maybe there's one other thing we should buy."

"Like what?"

Fry inclined his head to indicate the gun shop across the street.

"How about a handgun?"

"I don't think so."

"One would have come in handy last night," Fry reminded him.

"Maybe," Trapp said, "but I'll stick with the Sharps."

"Nobody says you have to give up the Sharps," Fry said. "I'm just saying—"

"I don't think so," Trapp said again. He didn't know exactly why he was refusing so firmly, unless it was a way of resisting progress. He wouldn't be able to do that for very long, because he *was* now living in a world that had progressed a long way since 1846.

He had seen only two small towns since leaving Huntsville. He knew that there was a lot more he was going to see that was going to surprise him, and perhaps even shock him.

The present would thrust itself upon him soon enough, but at the moment he just wanted to get his trek to his mountain under way, just him, his horse, and his Sharps, the way it used to be in the mountains.

"Are we ready to go?" Fry asked.

He looked at Fry, a young man who may or may not have been what he claimed to be. So far Fry had done nothing to make Trapp think ill, or different of him.

Many times in the mountains he had gone hunting with friends, or people who were simply partners. He wondered about them, and if any of them would still be around when he reached his destination.

For now Fry was both friend and partner, coming along for the ride.

It struck Trapp that this was going to be a long way to go just to come along for the ride.

"Yeah," he said, "we're ready, Fry."

During the trip he'd find out more about Fry, and Fry would find out more about him. When they reached the mountains, they *might* be friends—good friends, with no reservations on either side.

That remained to be seen.

Fry looked at Trapp riding alongside him and wondered about him. He certainly didn't act like a man over sixty should act. After all those years in Huntsville, he was still an imposing figure, still had pretty good reflexes, and—if Annie Bennett was any indication—was still attractive to women more than half his age.

Fry was curious about Trapp, but it was more than curiosity that drove him to join Trapp on his trek to his mountain.

Much more.

Maybe, at some point, he'd even tell Trapp the truth about that.

EIGHTEEN

Keller was angry.

He was in Littlesworth, a nothing, dustbowl of a town in a godforsaken section of Texas, and nothing but a job could have brought him there.

He'd arrived at the gates of Huntsville Prison only to find out that John Henry Trapp, through some clerical error, had been released two days early.

He'd been forced at that point to put his hunter's skills to work.

Very often in his business Keller put himself in his quarry's position, trying to figure out what the other man would do.

He decided that if he was John Henry Trapp, getting out of prison after twenty-five years, he'd want to stay away from large towns for the time being. That meant heading west, to Littlesworth, which was where he was now.

It only took some conversation making in the saloon for him to find out that he was right. Trapp had been there, and had been involved in an altercation during which he had killed two men.

When Keller first took the job, he'd been assured that he was going after an old man. These did not sound like the actions of an old man.

He took a moment to recall his initial meeting with Sam Train at his home in Denver. . . .

Keller walked up to the door of the big house and made use of the large brass knocker. He waited a few moments and was about to knock again when he heard the lock click and the door opened.

"Can I help you?" a well-dressed, balding man asked.

"Mr. Train?" Keller asked.

"No, sir," the man answered politely. "I am not Mr. Train. May I ask who you are and what your business is?"

"My name is Keller, and Mr. Train knows my business."

"Ah, yes, Mr. Keller," the man said, "we have been expecting you."

"Good," Keller said.

"Come in, please."

Keller entered and waited while the butler closed the door.

"This way, sir," the butler said, and led Keller down a long hall to a pair of glass French doors. The house was impressive, but Keller was not impressed with it or with the wealth that had built or bought it. Keller was not impressed by material things, he was only impressed by men—very *few* men.

The butler opened the doors and stepped in, then to the side.

"Mr. Keller, sir."

Keller was not yet in the room and he thought he heard a voice, but could not be sure. Apparently the butler had heard it, for he responded.

"Yes, sir," the man said, and then to Keller. "Please, come in."

Keller entered the room and found it oppressively hot. He immediately removed his jacket, revealing the gun he wore under his arm in a shoulder rig. It was his city gun, and he wore it when he was in Denver, or San Francisco, or New York, or anywhere a gun on the hip attracted undue attention.

"Sit down, Mr. Keller," he heard a whispery voice say. He looked around for the speaker and recoiled in shock that he immediately covered.

The man who had spoken was old—no, not old, *ancient!* He sat in a wheelchair with one blanket over his legs and another over his shoulders. His hair was the whitest Keller had ever seen, like snow, but it was thin and beneath it he could see a gleaming pink scalp.

The flesh of the man's face, instead of being wrinkled, was smooth and pink. The only wrinkles on the face were beneath the man's bloodless bottom lip, where there used to be a chin.

Keller would have guessed eighty, but even that might have been generous.

"Please," Sam Train said, "you must come closer or you will not hear me."

As it was, Keller didn't hear him, but he reacted to

the crooking, skeletal finger of one of the old man's hands.

Keller moved closer and sat in a well-stuffed chair.

"Oliver," Train said, "some brandy."

"Yes, sir."

Oliver—the butler—went to a sideboard and poured a glass snifter of brandy. He carried it over and handed it to Keller.

"None for you?" Keller asked Train.

"I would not be able to get it down," Train said.

Keller made a face and hid it behind the snifter.

"Would you like a cigar?" Train asked.

"Yes."

"Oliver?"

Oliver brought over a box of cigars and Keller took one. He passed it beneath his nose, enjoying the scent, and then lit it by a flame Oliver held. He took one puff and was sorry he had accepted. It was hot enough in there without smoking.

"Oliver," Train said, "the stones."

"Yes, sir."

Keller watched Oliver walk to a tub filled with water. He used a small pot to scoop some up and Keller could hear the ice clinking against the metal. Oliver then walked over to the pit and poured it in. The water struck a group of heated stones, and the result was a huge cloud of steam. The result was that the heat became even more oppressive.

"I apologize for the heat," Train said, "but I have very little blood left. Without it I would surely freeze to death."

"I understand."

Robert J. Randisi

"Remove your shirt if you must."

"If we get down to business," Keller said, opening his collar, "I won't be here that long." He took out a handkerchief and mopped the beads of sweat from his face and neck. He couldn't do anything about the rivulets of perspiration that were trickling down his back.

"Very well," Train said. "I want you to kill a man."

Keller looked at Oliver.

"Oliver can hear anything we say."

"Killing is my business, Mr. Train," Keller said. "You knew that when you sent for me."

"Yes," Train said, "but I want you to kill an old man. Have you any qualms about that?"

Keller shrugged. "None."

"This man has just about finished a twenty-five-year prison term in Huntsville Prison. He's getting out in a week."

"And you want me to kill him?" Keller asked. "Hasn't he been through enough?"

"No," Train said, "he has not. Twenty-five years ago he killed my son. I was not able to have him executed, but I *was* able to use my influence to get him sentenced to twenty-five years in prison."

"Why not have him killed in prison?" Keller asked.

"I considered it," Train said. "In fact, I had it tried twice, to no avail. I was about to have it done a third time when I realized that would be letting him off easy."

"So you decided to let him serve his entire sentence, and *then* have him killed."

"P-precisely," Train said.

It was clear that the old man was tiring.

"I—I'm sure he thinks I'm dead," Train said, "but I

114

refuse to die until he does. He won't be—be expecting someone like you—"

The old man stopped speaking and Oliver moved to his side. Train waved a hand and Oliver leaned over to hear what he had to say.

When he straightened up, Oliver said to Keller, "Do you accept?"

Keller looked at Train, who seemed semiconscious, and said, "Yes, with one condition."

"What condition?"

"I want to be paid in advance."

"Impossible," Oliver said.

"It's the only way I'll take the job," Keller said. He looked at Train and said, "No offense, Mr. Train, but you could die and I won't get paid."

"How do we know you won't take the money and not do the job?" Oliver asked.

Keller gave Oliver a hard stare, and the butler began to fidget.

"I'm sure Mr. Train checked me out before sending for me," Keller said. "I've never failed to carry out a job."

"I—I didn't mean—" Oliver said, but he stopped when the old man raised a hand like a claw and pulled on his sleeve. Oliver bent over so Train could say something in his ear, and then straightened.

"Mr. Train accepts your condition."

"I want to be paid in cash."

Oliver looked at Train, who dropped his chin. He had either nodded, or nodded off.

"Come with me," Oliver said. "I will give you what you need."

Keller rose and started to say something to Train, but Oliver stopped him.

"He won't hear you."

They went outside and Oliver closed the doors behind them.

"How old is he?"

"Eighty-nine."

"He looks older."

The butler paid Keller in cash, twenty-five thousand dollars, described John Henry Trapp, and supplied the mountain man's background.

He had been told that Trapp was about sixty-four, and had not expected any trouble. This should have been the easiest money he had ever made. He had been instructed to make sure that Trapp knew that Sam Train had sent him to kill him before he actually did it.

Because of the early release, and the story he'd heard about Trapp in Littlesworth, he was starting to think that the old mountain man might be more of a challenge than he'd thought. From what Oliver had told him, the mountain man had been formidable twenty-five years ago.

That was all right with Keller. His anger had faded and had been replaced by the old excitement that usually rose up when he began a hunt. He'd follow Trapp all the way to the Green River country if he had to, and kill him there.

Yes, that would be poetic justice. Kill him just when he reached his precious mountains.

Sam Train would like that.

If he lived long enough to find out about it.

Book Four

The Journey Begins

NINETEEN

John Henry Trapp had never seen land as flat as the Staked Plains of Texas.

And hot? Jesus, it was hot enough to fry bacon on his head, if he'd been bald. Hell, as far as he was concerned, it was even too hot to eat.

Though Fry didn't think so. Even when they stopped at midday to camp, Fry would take out the frying pan, build a fire, and fry up some bacon to go with the coffee. Trapp couldn't drink the coffee. The cold water they had put into their canteens a few miles back at the water hole had gone tepid already, but at least it quenched his thirst.

"How can you drink that?" he said to Fry, who was having his second cup of coffee.

"I like coffee," Fry said. "No, it's even worse than that. I *love* coffee. I've got to have my coffee."

"Your outsides are burning up in this sun, and now you want to burn up your insides as well?"

"Don't worry about it, Trapp," Fry said. "Here, have a slice of bacon."

"I don't know how you can eat that either," Trapp said.

"It's cooled off now," Fry said, putting the bacon into his mouth.

Trapp made a face and looked away. Something caught his eyes and he put down his canteen.

"What is it?" Fry asked.

"Have you had much experience with Indians?"

"Some," Fry said. "I've known a few, but they weren't plains Indians."

Fry looked where Trapp was looking and saw riders coming toward them. They were off a ways, but it was clear that they were Indians.

"What about you?" he asked.

"I've had experience with some of the mountain Indians," he said. "The Blackfeet, the Crow, the Shawnee. I don't know anything about these plains Indians."

"Comanches," Fry said.

"You can tell from here?"

"No, but that's what I hear they got around here, Comanches."

"Have you ever been to this part of Texas before?" Trapp asked.

"No."

"Are we near any towns?"

"I think there's a fort near here, Fort ... McAdams, or something like that."

"Which way?" Trapp asked.

"I asked around in Littlesworth," Fry said. "The fort should be about ten miles east of here."

"It's out of our way," Trapp said, "but maybe we should head for it. We could pick up some supplies and ask about the Indians in the area."

Fry looked again at the approaching Indians, who were still too small to make out clearly, and then started kicking out the fire.

"Let's go, Trapp," Fry said.

"I'm with you," Trapp said. He stood up and then grabbed his back and staggered.

"What's wrong?" Fry asked.

"Nothing," Trapp said. He rubbed the pain away from his lower back. Between sitting in the saddle and sitting on the hard ground, his back was killing him. "I just haven't spent this much time in the saddle in a lot of years."

They broke camp and saddled up, then took one more look back at the Indians.

"You think we can beat them to the fort?" Trapp asked.

Fry looked at Trapp and smiled.

"If you don't fall apart on me, old timer."

"I'll give you old timer," Trapp said. "Set the pace, you young whelp."

"You know," Fry said, "it's a good thing you ain't riding that fly bait you were riding when we met."

"If I was," Trapp said, "we wouldn't have to worry about *me* falling apart."

"All right," Fry said, "we'd better ride before we're up to our knees in Indians."

They started riding east, and Trapp hoped that the information Fry had gotten about Fort McAdams was right.

"They stopped."

Trapp turned and looked. Sure enough, the Indians, who had slowly been cutting into the gap between them, had suddenly stopped.

"Why?" Trapp wondered aloud.

There was a small rise ahead of them and Fry said, "Maybe they know something we don't know."

"Like what?" Trapp said.

"Let's keep going."

They rode up the rise, and as they topped it, they saw that fort.

"Like that," Fry said.

"Fort McAdams," Trapp said.

"We made it."

"Maybe . . ." Trapp said.

"What do you mean, maybe?"

"Well, even after we go in," Trapp said, looking behind him, "we've still got to come out again."

With that sobering thought between them they started for the front gates.

They were admitted to the fort and rode through it to the settlement behind it.

Fort McAdams settlement was larger than either of the towns Trapp had seen since he was released from Huntsville Prison. It was larger, and it was busier. The streets were teaming with people and wagons, and they had to stop once or twice as they rode down the main street toward the livery stable.

"Crowded, eh?" Fry asked.

"Yeah," Trapp said. He felt uneasy and he wondered if it showed.

"I was in San Francisco once," Fry said. "This is like one street in San Francisco."

"Is that right?" Trapp asked. "I don't think I'll be visiting San Francisco in the near future."

"Are you all right?" Fry asked.

"Yeah," Trapp said. "I'm just not used to being around this many people, that's all."

"Relax," Fry said. "People are people, whether there are five, fifty, or five hundred."

"Once a year," Trapp said, "in the mountains we would have a rendezvous."

"Rendezvous?"

"Yeah," Trapp said. "All of the trappers and hunters would get together with the buyers from the East, sell their skins, have contests—"

"Contests? What kind of contests?"

"Sharpshooting, wrestling, different things. We would do business and have fun."

"What's your point?"

"That's the only time I've ever been someplace where there were more than five or six people in one place at one time. Just that one time each year—and the last rendezvous took place five years before I went to prison."

"Just take it easy, Trapp," Fry said.

"I will," Trapp said. "I'll take it easy."

Trapp's heart was pounding and he felt closed in, but he fought the feelings of confinement away.

They reached the livery and gave their horses over to the liveryman.

"How many hotels are there in town?" Fry asked the liveryman.

"Two," the man said proudly. "We just opened the second one."

"Really?" Fry asked. "That's great. Which one would that be?"

"McAdams' House," the man said.

"McAdams' House?" Fry repeated. "That's a clever name for a hotel. What was the first hotel called?"

The liveryman grinned, showing gaps where teeth used to be, and said, "Hotel."

Fry looked at Trapp and said, "What do you say we try McAdams' House?"

Trapp didn't relish the walk back to the hotel, through the crowded streets, but what he wanted most now was to get into a hotel room, where he'd have enough space to breathe.

"Sure," he said. "Let's go."

He held his breath while they walked from the livery to the hotel. Beside him Fry was talking, but Trapp didn't hear a word he was saying. He came face-to-face with two men at one point and froze, but the look on his face made the two men go around him.

"Come on, Trapp," Fry said, putting his hand on his arm.

They reached McAdams' House and went inside, and Trapp released the breath he was holding.

"I'll get a room," Fry said.

"Two," Trapp said, his chest aching, "get two. I'll pay."

"I can pay for my own room, Trapp," Fry said. "I'll get two."

Fry got the two rooms and they went upstairs.

"You want to get something to eat?" Fry asked outside Trapp's room.

"In a little while," Trapp said. "Just give me . . . a little while."

"Sure, Trapp, sure," Fry said. "I'll come by for you later, eh?"

"Sure," Trapp said, "later."

Trapp went inside, shut the door behind him, and threw his saddlebags on the bed. He set the Sharps down and walked to the window. Outside on the street, people were still walking back and forth, civilians and soldiers; wagons were still going both ways. It was about three in the afternoon. He wondered how long it would be before the people began to thin out, before he dared to step outside of this room.

He sat on the bed. How the hell was he going to get along if being around people scared him. That's right, it *scared* him, and it choked him, and if he couldn't get over that . . .

Well, he didn't *have* to get over it. Once he got back to his mountain, he wouldn't have to worry about being around people.

They'd spend the one night here, buy some supplies, get some advice about the Indians, and then be on their way.

He lay back on the bed, enjoying the softness beneath him. He was warning himself about getting used to that when he drifted off to sleep.

Wendell Fry lay back on his bed and thought about Trapp. Being around people was really unnerving the older man. Fry could understand it. Even in Huntsville, Trapp probably wasn't as crowded as he had been walking on the street from the livery to here. For a man who was used to the space he had in the mountains, this many people would have to be scary.

Fry himself, he liked people. He liked the big cities, like San Francisco, even though he rarely got to them. The more the merrier, he thought, especially when some of the people were pretty ladies—*available* pretty ladies.

He thought about this new friendship with John Henry Trapp. The two of them were as alike as night and day. There was more than years between them. They had different likes and dislikes, and the only thing they had in common was . . . what?

They didn't have *anything* in common. Even their reasons for riding to Trapp's mountain were different.

Trapp was riding *to* something.

Fry was riding *away* from something.

TWENTY

Trapp woke a few minutes before Fry knocked on his door. In those few minutes he spoke harshly to himself about his problem. It was something he could live with, he told himself. People are people, Fry had said, and he was exactly right.

He could put up with it for one day.

When Fry knocked on the door, Trapp opened it.

"Are you all right?" Fry asked.

"Sure, Kid," Trapp said, "I'm fine."

"You want to go and get a drink, and then something to eat?"

"Yeah," Trapp said, "a drink sounds good."

"Okay," Fry said. "Let's get a drink, something to eat, and then we'll talk to someone about the Indians."

"And we can get going in the morning," Trapp said.

"Sure," Fry said, "we'll get going in the morning."

Trapp picked up his Sharps, stepped out into the hall, and pulled the door shut.

* * *

Nick Bodine thought a lot of himself.

He thought he was a great lover of women, and a great man with a gun. Not a *good* man with a gun, but a *great* man. He *knew* he was great with women, he had proven that over and over again, but he still had to prove to people that he was great with a gun.

Bodine had been looking for months for the opportunity to do that, and then it rode right into Fort McAdams, right down the center of the main street.

"You know who that is?" he asked the two men who were standing on the street with him. They had just come out of the saloon.

"Who?" Tom Masters asked.

"That one, riding in."

"The old guy?"

"No, stupid," Bodine said, "the guy with him."

"The young guy."

"Yeah, the young guy, genius," Bodine said. "You know who that is?"

"No, I don't know who it is."

"I seen him down in New Mexico, a couple of years ago," Bodine said. He looked at the other man, Sam Gorman. "You know who he is?"

"No, Nick," Gorman said with a shrug, "I don't know who he is."

"That's Kid Fry."

"Who?" Gorman asked.

"Oh yeah," Masters said, "I heard of him. He's supposed to be pretty good with a gun."

"Pretty good?" Bodine said. "Shit, I saw him take

two men at one time. *Two!* That takes more than a man who's *pretty* good."

"All right, Nick, all right," Masters said, "so he's great with a gun."

"That's right," Bodine said, "he's great, but I'm better."

"Sure you are, Nick," Masters said.

"No, I mean it," Bodine said. "I'm better, and I'm gonna prove it."

"When, Nick?"

"Today," Bodine said. "We don't know how long he's gonna be here, so I'll do it today . . . I'll do it later today."

"Hey, Nick," Gorman said.

"What?"

"If you was in New Mexico and saw him take two men, how come you didn't take him then?"

Bodine looked at Gorman and said, "Why don't you shut up?"

Trapp and Fry walked into the Lucky Spur Saloon and approached the bar.

"What can I get for you gents?" the bartender asked.

"Beer," Fry said. He looked at Trapp, who nodded and said, "Two beers."

"Coming up."

Trapp turned and looked the room over. It was a big saloon, and it was doing good business. During the walk over he'd allowed himself to breathe slowly, and now he felt as if he could actually stand being among this many people. As long as he knew they were leaving tomorrow, he could stand it.

"Here you go, gents," the bartender said. "Nice and cold, the way it's supposed to be."

"Thanks," Fry said.

Trapp turned and picked up his beer.

"Your friend here looks like he just came down from the mountains," the bartender said good-naturedly.

"He came down a long time ago," Fry said. "Now he's looking to go back up again."

"Well, enjoy the beer, gents. If you need more, just let me know."

"Thanks."

Fry looked the room over and saw a couple of poker games going. It was still too early for the house tables to be open.

"You feel like some poker, Trapp?"

"Not tonight, Kid," Trapp said. "You can try your hand, though."

"Maybe later," Fry said. One of the saloon girls came by and ran her hand over Fry's chest, and then kept going. "Maybe I'll try some of that later, too, but first we got to get something to eat."

"Yeah," Trapp said, "yeah, I am kind of hungry." He was surprised to find that he was hungry. Also, the knot in his stomach was gone.

They drank their beers and then Fry asked the bartender where a good place to eat was.

"There's a small restaurant just down the street; it's run by a woman named Maria. They've got great food there, just great."

"Okay, we'll try it," Fry said. "Thanks."

"You fellas passing through?"

"Yeah, we got herded this way by some Indians," Fry said.

"The Comanches," the man said knowingly. "Quanah Parker's braves."

"Quanah Parker?"

"Yeah. He's half white and he's their leader. How do you like that?"

"Half white, eh?"

"Yeah," the bartender said, "I even hear he's got blue eyes."

"A blue-eyed Indian."

"If you had a run-in with him, you'd better talk to the commanding officer at the fort, Major Fisher."

"Major Fisher," Fry said. "All right, we'll do that, but first we'll eat, huh?"

"Sure," the bartender said, "you've got to take care of the inner man first, right?"

"You're so right," Fry said.

"Let's go and eat," Trapp said. He was getting hungrier by the minute. "I'm starved."

"You wouldn't be so starved," Fry said, "if you had eaten some of my bacon."

They walked down the street to Maria's, unaware of the fact that they were being watched by three men across the street.

"Where are they going?" Gorman asked.

"They just got to town, where would you be going?" Bodine asked.

"I'd be looking for a whore," Gorman said.

"You're a damned animal," Bodine said. "They're looking for someplace to eat, probably Maria's."

Bodine and his friends had been in Fort McAdams for a month, and had eaten in Maria's many times.

"At least he'll have a good meal under his belt when I kill him," Bodine said.

TWENTY-ONE

"Well, at least we found out something," Fry said after they had ordered from a heavyset woman in her late forties. They assumed that she was Maria.

"Like what?"

"Quanah Parker," Fry said.

"The blue-eyed Comanche," Trapp said. "I've never seen an Indian with blue eyes."

"Neither have I. You curious?"

"Not enough to go out looking for him," Trapp said fervently. "After we eat we'd better go and talk to that major . . ."

"Fisher," Fry said. "I agree."

"Maybe we can get an escort part of the way."

"I doubt that," Fry said. "They've got enough to do out here besides escorting a couple of civilians, but we might be able to get some advice."

The woman came back with a pot of coffee and two cups.

"Your steaks will be ready in a moment," she told them.

"Don't forget," Fry said. "Rare."

"I won't forget."

It was actually early for dinner, but the small restaurant was full. Luckily, there was enough room between tables that Trapp didn't feel too crowded.

"How are you doing?" Fry asked.

"I'm all right," Trapp said. "It just takes some getting used to, you know?"

"How many men did you share your cell with in Huntsville?"

"Three others," Trapp said, "sometimes two."

"It must have been cramped."

"It was," Trapp said, "but there were only four of us at the most. It wasn't bad."

"I'll take your word for it," Fry said.

"Never been inside?"

Fry looked at Trapp for a moment before answering.

"Once or twice, for a night, when I was younger and thought that courage came out of a whiskey bottle, but never for any length of time."

"Good," Trapp said.

The woman returned bearing two huge plates. On each was a big slab of steak, a bunch of boiled potatoes, and some vegetables.

"I'll bring out some rolls."

"Thank you," Fry said.

As the woman left, Trapp said, "You've got to be the politest sonofabitch I ever met. You 'thank you' to everybody for everything."

"You stay out of trouble that way," Fry said. "Nobody can ever question your tone."

"Have you had trouble with that?"

Fry put his elbows on the table.

"About the same time I learned that courage doesn't come in a whiskey bottle I learned that if somebody wants to start a fight with you, it's real hard to do when you're being polite."

"You seemed to have learned a lot for one so young."

"I'm not that young," Fry said. "I'm twenty-five, but I feel older."

"That's funny," Trapp said.

"Why?"

"I'm sixty-four and I feel younger."

"Maybe we can meet halfway somewhere."

"No," Trapp said, "don't give away any of your youth. Enjoy every minute of it, because you never know when someone is going to try and take it away from you."

"I live with that, Trapp," Fry said. "Any minute some fella who fancies himself with a gun could come through that door and try for me. At least when they put you away, you stayed alive. My way, I could end up dead very young."

"Sometimes I wished I *was* dead," Trapp said, "but then I realized that no matter where you are or what you're doing, life is precious. So I hung on, and I beat the bastards."

"Here's to beating the bastards," Fry said, holding up his coffee cup.

"Beating the bastards," Trapp said.

* * *

Keller hated the Staked Plains. He'd spent some time there over the years, and liked it less and less each time. This time, however, he regarded it as a rainbow, and at the end of it maybe there was a pot of gold. Although he'd gotten his money already, he wouldn't feel that it was truly his until he did what he was paid to do—kill John Henry Trapp.

Two days, at the most he was two days behind them. It didn't seem so much when you thought of it in days rather than hours. Two days sounded like a lot less than forty-eight hours.

Two days.

"Why don't we just go in and tell him to come out onto the street?" Sam Gorman asked.

"Quiet," Bodine said.

"I mean, instead of standing out here waiting for him. Are we even gonna do it when they come out?"

"Shut up, Gorman," Bodine said.

Gorman gave Bodine a wounded look, but fell silent.

"What about it, Nick?" Masters asked.

"I want to watch them for a while," Bodine said. "Maybe they'll split up."

"Come on," Masters said, "an old man with an old buffalo gun can't be that much trouble."

"We'll watch them and wait, Tom," Bodine said, "unless you want to go in there yourself and make a try for Kid Fry yourself."

"Not me, Nick," Masters said. "I'll back your play, but I got no hankerin' to go up against him myself."

"Smart," Bodine said, "real smart. You just back my play, Tom, and everything will turn out fine."

From where Fry was sitting, he could look out the front window.

"We've got some company," he said to Trapp.

"Who?"

Trapp was sitting with his back to the door and started to turn around.

"Don't turn," Fry said, arresting the movement. "Three jaspers, standing across the street."

"What makes you call them company?"

"They followed us here from the saloon."

Trapp frowned, chewing on a potato.

"For what?"

"If I had to guess," Fry said, "I'd say they were looking for trouble."

"Do we look like we've got something worth taking?" Trapp asked.

"Well, we do have some money on us, thanks to you, but that's not what they're after."

"What *are* they after?"

"Me, I'd say," Fry said. "One of them might have recognized me."

Trapp frowned again and stopped chewing.

"I thought you said you had a *little* bit of a reputation."

"I do," Fry said, "but that doesn't mean I couldn't have been in the same place at the same time with somebody, and they remember."

"So what do we do?"

"Nothing," Fry said. "We finish eating and go and talk to the army."

"What about them?"

"They'll watch and wait for a while," Fry said.

"How do you know?"

"It's what I'd do."

"You think they're as smart as you are?"

"God," Fry said, "I hope not."

TWENTY-TWO

After they had finished eating, they complimented the woman—who was indeed Maria—and left the restaurant, heading for the fort.

"Are they still there?" Trapp asked.

"Still there," Fry said, "but I doubt that they'll follow us into the fort."

As it turned out, he was correct. As they passed through the gates into the fort, the three men behind them stopped and simply watched.

"I told you," Fry said, "they'll watch and wait. They might even wait and see if we split up."

"In that case," Trapp said, "we won't."

"Well," Fry said thoughtfully, "we can talk about that later."

"They went into the fort!" Sam Gorman said.

"I can see, Sam," Bodine said.

"What do we do now?" Masters asked.

"What the hell are they going into the fort for?" Gorman said.

"Maybe they had a run-in with some Indians," Bodine said. "If that's the case, they'll just talk to the commander and come right back out."

"And we'll be waiting?" Gorman asked.

"Waiting and watching."

"Shit," Gorman said, "I'm getting damned tired of waiting."

"If you're so tired of waiting, then you can move on, Sam," Bodine said. "If you're staying with me, then just try keeping your trap shut for a change."

"Jeez, Nick, you don't have to—sure I'm staying—I was just—"

Masters closed his hand over Gorman's elbow to attract his attention and then shook his head to shut him up.

It worked.

"And your name is?" the lieutenant asked.

Trapp had presented himself at the commanding officer's office, and Lieutenant Avery had introduced himself as the major's aide.

"My name is Trapp, and we'd like to talk to the major about some Indians."

"What Indians?"

"That's what we'd like to talk to him about," Trapp said. "We're not quite sure what Indians."

"Wait here, please," the young lieutenant said. "I'll see if the major has time to see you."

"Thank you," Trapp said, thinking about what Fry had told him about being polite.

As they had reached the commanding officer's office, Fry had suggested that maybe he should stay outside.

"You know, Kid," Trapp said, "we're going to have to have another talk about this reputation of yours."

"Sure," Fry said, "maybe when we get to your mountain, huh, Trapp?"

"We'll see."

Trapp waited a few minutes and then the lieutenant came back out.

"The major will see you now."

As Trapp stepped into the room the major, a white-bearded, white-haired man stood up and stared at him curiously. Trapp made a mental note to buy some new clothes later. He was still wearing what the people at Huntsville had given him, and up to now it hadn't made much difference. It was time for a change, though.

"Major," he said, approaching the desk and shaking hands, "thank you for seeing me."

"My aide said something about Indians," the major said. The man's handshake was not that of a leader, Trapp thought. It was too limp. "Have you had some dealings with Quanah Parker?"

"Well, sir, my partner and I aren't quite sure who we encountered," Trapp said. "We were—well, *stalked*, I suppose is the word, as far as this fort—"

"How close to the fort did they follow?"

"That rise just south of the gate? They followed us to that point—"

"It would have to be Quanah's men, then," the major said. "They're the only ones with the nerve to get that close."

"Major, we were wondering if you might not have

some suggestions as to how we might, ah, avoid them when we leave come morning."

"Avoid them?" the major said. "There's only one way to do that, sir."

"And what's that?"

"*Don't* leave."

Trapp laughed shortly and said, "We can't do that, sir. We have to leave."

"Then you'll just have to outrun them, mister," the major said, "although if they want you bad enough they'll ride all day until they ride you down. It's either that or wait until our next supply train comes in. You can leave with them."

"When will that be?"

"About a month or so."

"You're not being very encouraging, Major."

"I'm sorry," the major said, "but I'd rather tell you the truth than coddle you with some story."

"I see," Trapp said. "I appreciate that. I don't suppose you'd be able to, uh, supply us with some kind of escort—"

"Impossible, unless you're carrying supplies for the government, or have women and children who are in danger?"

"Neither one, I'm afraid," Trapp said.

"Then I guess we don't have much else to discuss, sir. Good day."

"Yeah," Trapp said, forgetting about being polite, "it was nice talking to you, too."

Outside Fry said, "So? What happened?"

"Nothing," Trapp said. "He says we either stay here

142

or take our chances out there, trying to outrun them."

"Not much of a choice," Fry said.

"Kid, you can stay here and wait for the supply train, and then leave with them."

"And you?"

"Me? I've been away from my mountains too long as it is," Trapp said. "I'll be leaving in the morning."

"Well, I'll be leaving with you, then," Fry said.

"Maybe we won't even meet up with them again," Trapp said.

"There's always that possibility," Fry said.

They started walking toward the back gate.

"Our friends are probably still out there waiting for us," Fry said. "Don't pay them any mind."

"What if they—"

"They won't," Fry said. "It isn't time yet."

They walked out the back gate and sure enough the three men were standing off to one side, watching them. Trapp didn't turn his head, but he could see them out of the corner of his eye.

"There's another possibility," Fry said.

"What's that?"

They began to walk through town, and the three men fell in behind them.

"Maybe there are some others in the same predicament as we are. Maybe they want to leave town, but don't dare."

"So?"

"So, if there are enough of them we could all leave together," Fry said. "A small show of force might persuade the Indians to leave us be."

"I guess that is a possibility," Trapp said, but his

tone clearly showed that he wasn't in favor of it.

Fry looked at Trapp and said, "So what's wrong with that?"

"I don't know," Trapp said. "Maybe old habits die hard, but I never used to make it a rule to travel with strangers. You never knew what they really wanted."

"Well, we'll have to decide where the least risk is," Fry said. "Let's talk about it over another beer."

"Another beer sounds good."

"Where are they going now?" Tom Masters said.

"Looks like they're headed for the saloon again," Bodine said.

"Good," Gorman said, "I could use a beer."

Bodine looked at Gorman and said, "I can hardly believe it."

"What?" Gorman asked. "What did I do now?"

"Something I would never have expected of you, Sammy," Bodine said.

"What?"

"You came up with an idea."

"I did?" Gorman said, sounding pleased with himself—then he frowned, looked at Masters and Bodine, and said, "What is it?"

TWENTY-THREE

Trapp and Fry got themselves a beer and found a table against the wall for themselves. Fry sat with his back to the wall, something Trapp noticed that he always did.

"Why do you always sit like that?" he asked.

"Like what?"

"With your back to the wall?"

Fry sipped his beer and put it down.

"So no one can ever come up behind me."

"Do you expect that?"

"Why else would I sit this way?"

"It must be a terrible way to live," Trapp said, "always expecting someone to sneak behind you and put a bullet in you."

"I don't *always* expect it," Fry said, "but it could happen. Why take chances, right?"

"Oh, right," Trapp said. He wondered why he suddenly developed an itch between his shoulder blades.

Suddenly, he wondered if the old man, Sam Train,

was still alive. And if he was, would he just forget about Trapp? That was unlikely. If he was still alive, he probably knew the exact date that Trapp was getting out of Huntsville.

Maybe Trapp should also start sitting with his back to the wall.

"What's on your mind?" Fry asked.

Trapp told him.

"How old would this Train be by now?"

Trapp shrugged.

"In his eighties, I guess, maybe ninety."

"Probably too old and senile to care that you were getting out," Fry offered.

"Maybe."

"Where did he live?"

"Denver."

"I guess we could check it out by telegraph," Fry said, "if you're interested."

Trapp didn't answer.

"If he is alive, you think he'd send someone after you?"

Again, Trapp shrugged.

"I'm sure he tried to have me killed inside a few times," Trapp said. "Why not outside?"

"The way to do it would be to hire someone to kill you," Fry said. "A gunman."

"Like you?"

Fry stared at Trapp.

"Is that what you think?" he asked. "That I'm here to kill you?"

Fry seemed genuinely offended, and Trapp was sorry for what he'd said.

"No, I only meant—"

"I may have a reputation with a gun, Trapp," Fry went on heatedly, "but I've never been a hired killer. That's not my style."

"All right," Trapp said. "I'm sorry. I believe you."

"I hope you do."

"I do. Okay?"

"Okay," Fry muttered, but Trapp could tell the younger man wasn't just going to forget it.

They sat and nursed their beers in silence, each alone with his own thoughts, and Fry finally broke the silence.

"You know them fellas that were following us?"

"Yeah?"

"One of them's been at the bar for a while, watching us."

Trapp started to turn but stopped himself.

"Just watching?"

"That's all."

"Maybe we should go over and have a talk with him."

"Maybe," Fry said. "I tell you what—why don't you get up and get us another couple of beers."

"Me? I'm no hand with a gun, Fry."

"I don't want you to shoot him," Fry said. "Fact of the matter is, you're pretty scary-looking, Trapp. Let's see how he reacts."

Trapp stared at Fry, mulling over the remark that he was "scary" looking, and then said, "Well, all right."

He stood up and started walking to the bar.

There were a lot of men at the bar and at first he

didn't know which one was watching them, but it didn't take a genius to figure it out. Almost everyone watched Trapp, because even as thin as he had become in prison, he was still of imposing height. But one fella, medium height and sort of weasily looking, suddenly developed a bad case of nerves. His eyes darted around the room, he licked his lips, and he started to sweat.

Trapp altered his course and walked right toward the man. The man didn't know whether to bolt and run or stand his ground. Finally he turned to face the bar, put his elbows on it, and hunched his shoulders.

Trapp reached the bar, elbowed his way between the nervous man and another man, and told the bartender, "Two beers."

"Comin' up."

While he waited, Trapp looked at the man on his right through the mirror, and then at the nervous man on the left. The man was fighting to keep his eyes down on his drink, but finally he raised them and looked into the mirror. He saw Trapp looking at him and for a moment Trapp thought he *was* going to run. Hastily, the man lowered his eyes and kept them there.

The bartender came with the two beers. Trapp thanked him, picked them up, and turned to walk away. The move startled the nervous man and he jerked, his arm knocking one of the beers from Trapp's hand. Some of the beer went on Trapp, but most of it went on the nervous man, who leaped back from the bar as if he'd been scalded.

"Hey—" Trapp said.

"I'm sorry!" the man said quickly. He shook his hands, trying to shake the wet beer from them. "Hey, my fault," he went on, "I—I'm just clumsy. I'll—I'll buy you another one."

He signaled the bartender, who put another beer on the bar for Trapp. Trapp picked it up and looked at the other man hard.

"Thanks," he finally said.

"Hey, no problem," the man said, the front of his shirt soaked with beer. "My fault, right?"

"If I was you," Trapp said, "I'd be careful—*real* careful."

"Huh? Oh, sure," the man said. It was clear he didn't quite know exactly what Trapp was talking about. "Sure thing, mister."

Trapp took the beers and walked back to the table.

"Nice performance," Fry said. "Spilling the beer on him was real smart."

"That was his fault," Trapp said, "not mine. That's one very nervous man."

"Yeah," Fry said, "and he's heading for the door like a scared rabbit."

Trapp turned just in time to see the man scurry out the door.

"Now what?" he asked Fry.

"Now we wait," Fry said. "We just wait."

Outside, Sam Gorman hurried over to where Nick Bodine and Tom Masters were standing.

"What happened to you?" Masters asked. "You look white as a ghost."

Robert J. Randisi

"You're all wet," Bodine said. "What is that?"

"Beer," Gorman said. "That big fella spilled it all over me."

"On purpose?" Bodine asked.

"Well of course on purpose," Gorman said. "He knows, Bodine."

"Knows what?"

"That I was watching him!" Gorman said. "Why else would he spill beer on me?"

"Maybe you did it," Bodine said. "Maybe you got scared and spilled it all over yourself."

"You're damned right I'm scared," Gorman said. "You don't know how big that sonofabuck is until he's standing right next to you!"

"And what about Kid Fry?" Bodine asked.

"He just stayed at his table and watched."

"Yeah," Bodine said, nodding. "He sent the big fella over to scare you."

"Well, he did."

"Did he talk to you?"

"Yeah," Gorman said, his eyes widening. "He said if he was me, he'd be real careful."

"Sure," Bodine said again, nodding.

"Well?" Gorman asked.

"Well what?" Bodine said.

"Are we?"

"Are we what?"

Exasperated, Gorman said, "Are we gonna be careful?"

"Oh, yeah," Bodine said thoughtfully, "we're gonna be real careful, just like the man said."

"What are we gonna do, Nick?" Masters asked.

Bodine looked at Masters and said, "Come on, we're going in."

"What if it's them?" Trapp asked.

"Them . . . what?" Fry asked.

"What if it's them that Sam Train sent to kill me?" Trapp asked.

"No sense in wondering about that until we find out whether or not Train is still alive, is there?" Fry asked. "They might just be after me."

"Well then, let's find out."

"I doubt the telegraph office will be open at this time," Fry said. "We'll just have to wait until morning to check that out. We'll do it just before we leave."

"We'll have to wait for an answer," Trapp reminded him.

Fry shrugged and said, "You're calling the shots, Trapp. Do we wait for an answer, or get moving?"

Trapp didn't hesitate.

"We'll wait," he said, even though he didn't relish spending another day in Fort McAdams. "We might as well find out one way or the other."

Fry looked past Trapp at that point, to the entrance, and said, "We may find out even sooner than we thought."

TWENTY-FOUR

"Steady," Fry said to Trapp. "Let's wait until they make their intentions clear."

"We could be dead by then," Trapp said urgently.

"Easy," Fry said. "I can kill any two of them before they clear leather."

"You're sure of that?"

Fry took his eyes off the three men who had entered the saloon just long enough to fire Trapp a confident look when he said, "Oh, yes."

Fry looked again at the three men and asked Trapp, "Can you handle the other one?"

Trapp hesitated just a moment before saying, "Sure."

"Nice and easy now, just slide your chair sideways a bit and put your hand on your Sharps."

The Sharps was leaning against the table, with Trapp's body between it and the three men. He slid his chair around as Fry had said and placed his hand on the barrel of the gun. From his new position he could see the three of them.

"No matter what position they take up," Fry said, "you take the one on your left. Got it?"

"I've got it."

"Don't move until they do."

"Right."

Trapp was nervous. He'd killed men before—even before he killed Sam Train's son—but he'd never had to do it under these conditions.

The three men fanned out, and it was clear that the two on the ends were taking their cue from the one in the center. Fry studied the man, but was sure he didn't know him from anywhere.

The others in the saloon gradually became aware that something was developing, and conversation died down to a low hum.

"You're Kid Fry," the man in the center finally said.

"So?" Fry said.

"I hear you're pretty good with a gun."

"So," Fry said again.

"I'm here to find out."

"Just you, or all three?" Fry asked.

"Just me."

"Then tell your friends to leave."

"You've got a friend," the man said. "They'll stay just to keep an eye on him."

"My friend's a harmless old man, mister."

Trapp gave Fry a quick look of annoyance, but then went back to watching the man on his left. His hand on the barrel of his Sharps was slick with perspiration.

"Stand up, Fry," the man said.

"What's your name?" Fry asked.

"What's that matter?"

"Come on," Fry said, "you know you want all these people to know your name. Why else would you be doing this than to build yourself a reputation? Besides, I don't like killing a man without knowing his name."

"You sure you're gonna kill me?"

"Son," Fry said, even though the other man was at least five years older than he was, "I'm not only gonna kill you, I'm gonna kill one of your friends, and *my* friend is gonna take care of the other one."

Trapp's man was the one who had spilled the beer, and the mountain man could see that he had gone beyond nervous all the way to scared. He was so scared he didn't know whether to watch his leaders, Fry, or Trapp, and his eyes were bouncing around in his head as he tried to watch all three.

"My name's Nick Bodine, Fry," Bodine said, "and you're a dead man. Stand up."

"I'll sit," Fry said. "You go ahead and make your move—or turn around, walk out, and keep on living."

A flicker of doubt crossed Bodine's face, but he pushed it away—Fry could *see* him doing it—and the man went for his gun.

Fry drew from his seated position and shot Bodine in the chest.

As Bodine drew, so did his friend on the right. Fry fired again, catching the man in the belly.

Trapp snatched his Sharps up, laid it across his lap,

and pulled the trigger. The ball hit the nervous man in the chest before the man could decide to draw.

Fry stood up now and walked over to check the three bodies. When he was sure they were dead, he ejected the spent shells from his gun and replaced them with live ones. That done, he holstered his gun. Trapp took the hint and hurriedly took up his powder horn to reload.

Fry looked at the bartender and asked, "You got a sheriff in this town?"

"Sure do," the man said, "Sheriff Del Keeper. He's a good man."

"Is he an understanding man?"

"He'll listen," the bartender said, "but he's gonna make his own mind up."

Fry looked at Trapp and was about to say something when the door to the saloon opened and a man with a badge walked in. Behind him were two soldiers holding rifles. They must have been passing by and been commandeered by the lawman.

Sheriff Del Keeper had his gun out, and looked as if he knew how to use it.

"What the hell—" he said, looking down at the bodies. He looked up at Fry then, who slowly lifted his hand away from his gun.

"This can be explained, Sheriff," Fry said.

"Good," Keeper said. "Why don't we go over to my office and see if we can't work on it?"

TWENTY-FIVE

"Did you have to be so truthful?" Fry asked.

"Excuse me," Trapp said, "but somehow, over the past twenty-five years, I've gotten into the habit of not lying to the law."

"What were you, some kind of model prisoner?"

"As a matter of fact—"

"All right, all right, never mind."

The bone of contention between them was the fact that when the sheriff had asked Trapp where they'd come from, he had answered honestly. Now the sheriff would probably check back with Littlesworth and Portsville and would find out that they had been involved with killings in each place.

"*We* know that it's just coincidence," Fry said, "but how do you think it's going to look to a lawman?"

"We can't help it if we attract trouble," Trapp said.

"That's all we have attracted since you got out of prison, and since we met."

"Well, this one obviously wasn't my fault," Trapp said. "They were after you!"

"And those two in Littlesworth?" Fry asked.

"They were ragging me, but you invited yourself into that one."

"And Portsville?"

"Some sore losers at poker," Trapp said.

"And we were partners by then, so I had to take a hand and save your ass."

"I was doing fine."

"Yeah, with that one-shot Sharps."

"It didn't do too badly tonight," Trapp said. "Maybe I saved *your* ass."

"Yeah," Fry said, "maybe."

Fry had been resting his face between the bars that were separating his cell from Trapp's. He looked at Trapp curiously now.

"Hey, how you holding up?"

Trapp looked up at the bars, then the ceiling, and finally the window. It was almost daylight, and they'd been there all night. Trapp had not been able to sleep. He was afraid he'd wake up and find himself back at Huntsville Prison.

"Well, I'm not real *happy* with my room, but I guess I'm holding up okay."

"It's not gonna work in our favor if the sheriff finds out you just got out of Huntsville," Fry said. He frowned at Trapp and asked, "You didn't tell him that, did you?"

"No," Trapp said.

"Well," Fry said, "luckily since we been traveling you've gotten rid of that prison pallor, so maybe he won't guess."

At that point, the door to the sheriff's office opened and the lawman came through. He had the keys in his hand and unlocked each of their cells in turn.

"Come out front when you get yourselves together," he said, and went back to his office.

Trapp and Fry picked up their shirts and left the cells. They followed the sheriff into the office.

Sheriff Del Keeper had Fry's gun and Trapp's Sharps on top of his desk. The sheriff had seated himself behind his desk and was rolling a cigarette. He was in his forties, with slate gray hair and a bushy mustache. He was starting to go thick around the middle, but still looked like a man who enjoyed the authority he held, and was confident in his ability to handle it.

"I checked you boys out."

"And?" Fry said.

"You've had quite a string of bad luck—or has it been good luck? Three shootings in three weeks, and not a scratch on either of you."

"We didn't start any of them, Sheriff," Trapp said.

"Oh, don't worry," Keeper said. "I got the stories from Littlesworth and Portsville. You fellas just seem to attract trouble, don't you?"

Neither Trapp nor Fry answered.

"All right," Keeper said. "Pick up your iron and go and attract it somewhere else."

"What does that mean?" Fry asked.

"I want you out of Fort McAdams."

"We only came here to get away from some Indians," Fry said.

"Well, I wouldn't wish you two on many people, but maybe your brand of luck can do some damage to Quanah Parker."

"We have to send a telegraph message before we leave, Sheriff," Fry said.

"And we have to wait for an answer."

"How long will that take?" Keeper asked.

"We're hoping only one extra day," Fry said. "We're eager to get going, Sheriff, even if it means trying to outrun Quanah and his boys."

"All right," Keeper said, rubbing his jaw, "I guess we can stand you for one more day—but stay out of trouble."

"That's always our intention, Sheriff," Trapp said, picking up his Sharps.

"That's a beautiful weapon, Trapp," the sheriff said. "It looks well cared for."

"It has been."

"It made a hole in that fella you could have driven a wagon through."

"That was the chance that fella took," Fry said, buckling his gunbelt on.

Keeper stood up, straightening to his height of better than six feet.

"I know your reputation, Fry."

Trapp looked at Fry, who didn't comment.

"Don't look to add to it here."

"Killing those three men wouldn't add to anyone's reputation, Sheriff," Fry said, adjusting his gunbelt so that it sat just right. "In fact, it was the other way around."

"Did you know those three, Sheriff?" Trapp asked.

"Yes," Keeper said. "They'd been here about a month now. Hadn't caused any trouble—until now."

"Well, I'm sorry to have been the cause of it," Fry said.

"A hazard in your profession, eh?"

"My profession?" Fry asked. "You don't know what my profession is, Sheriff. You might assume, but you don't know."

"No," Keeper admitted, "maybe I don't. All right, Mr. Fry, Mr. Trapp. I hope the accommodations were to your liking."

"My compliments," Fry said wryly. "Is the telegraph office open this early?"

"Not for a couple of hours."

"And the restaurant, Maria's?"

Keeper shook his head.

"Not for another hour."

"Well," Fry said, "I guess we'll just have to wait for our breakfast."

"I'm sorry to release you so early," Keeper said. "Another hour and I would have served you breakfast in your cells."

"That's all right, Sheriff," Trapp said. "We'd just as soon fetch it ourselves."

"Good morning, Sheriff," Fry said.

Keeper nodded and watched Trapp and Fry walk out.

On the boardwalk in front of the office, Trapp paused and took a deep breath.

"Okay?" Fry asked.

"*Now* I am, yes," Trapp said.

"Hungry?"

"Starved."

"Why don't we go to the hotel and change into fresh clothes," Fry said, "and then go to breakfast."

"I don't have any fresh clothes," Trapp reminded him.

"Yeah," Fry said, wrinkling his nose, "I've been meaning to talk to you about that, Trapp."

TWENTY-SIX

They returned to the hotel so that Fry could change into fresh clothes.

Maria's was among the earliest of the businesses to open. They went there and had breakfast while waiting for the telegraph office and the general store to open.

"We'll get you a pair of jeans and some shirts at the general store," Fry said, "and then we'll try the telegraph office."

"Let's try the telegraph office first," Trapp said, "and while waiting for the answer we can look for the new clothing."

"Sure, okay," Fry said. "That makes sense."

They finished their leisurely breakfast and found the telegraph office open.

"Sam Train, right?" Fry asked.

"That's right."

Fry composed the telegram and read it to Trapp.

"Who are we sending it to?" Trapp asked.

That stumped Fry for a moment, but then he said, "I might as well send it to the Denver Police Department. I'll just say that I heard that Sam Train had been killed, and we'll see what happens."

Trapp waited outside while Fry sent the telegram, and endured the unpleasant looks that passing women gave him. He was going to have to get some new clothes.

Fry came out and said, "All right, it's sent. If Train was, or is, the big shot you said he was, we should get a prompt reply."

A woman walked by and gave Trapp a long, disapproving look.

"Let's get you those new clothes," Fry said.

"Good idea."

They went to the general store and bought the largest-sized shirts and jeans they had.

"What about a hat?" the clerk asked.

"Up to now you could use the sun on your face," Fry said. "Maybe now it's time for a hat."

"What kind?" Trapp asked.

"I have several different kinds," the clerk said.

Trapp looked at the hats and didn't like any of them. He finally settled on the same flat-crowned Stetson that Fry wore, only one less fancy. Fry's had a band of silver around the crown. Trapp took one that was plain.

They went back to the hotel with the clothes and Fry said, "Time for a bath."

"A what?"

Fry laughed and said, "A bath."

"Is that really necessary?" Trapp asked.

"It is as long as we're here," Fry said.

"We're only going to be here another day."

"If you're going to put on new clothes, you should take a bath."

Trapp didn't like the idea—that was obvious.

"Didn't you take baths in the mountains?"

"Sure, every so often."

"How often?"

"Eight, maybe nine times."

"A month?"

"A month!" Trapp said, shaking his head. "Eight or nine times a *year*."

"Yeah, well," Fry said, "I take a few more than that. I really think this is a must."

Fry went to the clerk and asked where the bathhouse was. When he had directions, he went back to Trapp.

"Come on," he said, "I'll protect you."

"From what?"

"From the big bad water."

"I don't need to be led by the hand," Trapp said.

"All right," Fry said. He told Trapp where the bathhouse was. "I won't have to come back and check on you, will I?"

"I'll take a bath," Trapp said, "but this one's going to last a while."

"Fine," Fry said, smiling.

Trapp went around behind the desk and down a

long hallway to where the bathtubs were. There were three, and they were all available.

"Can I help you?" a man asked. He was a small, wiry man in his late fifties.

"I . . . want to take a bath."

"Hot or cold?"

"Hot?" Trapp said. Anytime he'd taken a bath in the mountains it had always been in a spring, or a lake. In prison when they bathed, it was with cold water. He had never had a hot bath, not even with Annie Bennett.

"Yeah, hot or cold?" the man said. "You got a choice."

"If I have a choice," Trapp said, "I'll take a hot one."

"Okay," the man said. "Get undressed and grab some soap and a towel. I'll fill the tub."

When the tub was filled, the man left and Trapp tested the water with his toe. It was scalding, but if he was going to take his first hot bath, he wanted to take it while the water was *very* hot. He forced himself to submerge completely, and after a few moments his entire body felt . . . soothed.

He hadn't felt this good in years.

Fry was waiting in the lobby and just when he thought something might have happened—could Trapp have drowned?—Trapp came walking out. He was dressed in his new clothes, and he was *clean*.

"What happened?" Fry asked.

"What do you mean?"

"You were in there a long time."

Trapp looked embarrassed.

"Well, if I was going to take a bath, I wanted to do it right."

"You old fraud," Fry said, grinning. "You enjoyed it, didn't you?"

"Well . . . I've never had a *hot* bath before," Trapp said. "It was . . . relaxing."

"A bath and some new clothes make all the difference," Fry said. "You look . . . different. One more thing would make the picture perfect."

"What's that?"

"A shave and a haircut."

Trapp poked Fry in the chest with a rigid forefinger and said, "Don't push your luck."

They went outside and the first women who walked past nodded at them pleasantly.

"See?" Fry said. "Now you look more human."

"What did I look like before?"

Fry shrugged and said, "A mountain man."

"Well," Trapp said, "I sure wouldn't want to look like one of them, would I?"

TWENTY-SEVEN

For the rest of the morning and all of the afternoon, they awaited a reply to the telegram. They passed the time by getting two chairs from inside the hotel and sitting on the boardwalk outside.

"Sitting in front of the telegraph office would be pushing it, just a little," Fry said.

"This is all right," Trapp said. "I'd rather be sitting here than trying to walk around. How can you stand being among this many people?"

"Well, I grew up around a lot of people, you know. I can understand your feelings, though."

Trapp fell silent and stayed that way.

"What's it like in the mountains?" Fry asked.

"It's quiet," Trapp said. "God, sometimes it's so quiet that all you can *hear* is the wind." Trapp's eyes became vague, as if he wasn't looking at anything in particular—or at something only he could see. "Sometimes the wind is all you hear for days, for weeks—unless it's an animal. You know, I've gone as long as six months without seeing another living soul."

"How could *you* stand that?" Fry said. "I need to see people every day."

"Wait," Trapp said. "Wait until you get to my mountain. You'll see what I mean. The air is like nothing you've ever breathed. The snow caps are like . . . like what pearls probably look like." Trapp looked at Fry and said, "I've never seen pearls, but they couldn't possibly be any more beautiful."

"I don't know," Fry said. "I've never seen pearls either."

"And the water," Trapp went on. "So clear, so damned cold that it brings every inch of your body to life."

Trapp put his head back and closed his eyes. Fry was about to do the same when he saw Sheriff Keeper coming their way.

"Here comes the law," he said.

Trapp opened his eyes and said, "Now what?"

They watched while the lawman drew closer.

"Taking it easy, I see," Keeper said, reaching them.

"Just doing what we said we'd do, Sheriff," Fry said, "staying out of trouble."

"I just got a telegram from Denver," the sheriff said. He took a piece of paper out of his pocket and read from it. "Sam Train alive and well. Please investigate threat." There was more, but that was all Keeper read to them.

"Why did you get that message?" Trapp asked.

"What threat?" Fry asked.

"That's what Denver wants to know," Keeper said. "It seems this Sam Train is a very important man in Denver, and has been for a long, long time. Why would you, Mr. Fry, write to the Denver Police and ask if he was dead?"

Fry shrugged and said, "Curiosity."

"And that's all?"

"That's it."

"There was no threat here?"

"Why would I threaten the man?" Fry asked. "I don't even know him."

"Then why would you be concerned about his health?"

"I told you," Fry said, "curiosity."

"Let me tell you something, Fry," Keeper said, putting his boot up on the boardwalk and leaning on his knee, "if you heard anything about a threat, or a planned attempt on Sam Train's life, Denver would really like to hear about it."

"I don't know anything, Sheriff Keeper," Fry said. "I swear I don't." He raised his right hand to give the oath strength.

"All right," Keeper said, straightening up. "I had an obligation to ask. I'll respond to Denver and tell them they have nothing to worry about."

Trapp watched the sheriff walk away and said, "I wish I could say the same for us."

"Why do you say that?"

"If he sends a telegram to Denver and mentions *my* name," Trapp said, "then if Train wasn't on my trail already he will be—mine and yours."

* * *

The sheriff went to the telegraph office and composed a short message:

CHIEF COLE, DENVER POLICE,
    QUESTIONED FRY AND TRAPP. NO CAUSE
FOR ALARM.
                        SHERIFF KEEPER

Satisfied that he had discharged his obligation to a fellow lawman, Keeper left and headed for the saloon.

Keller was furious.

Just when he knew he was closing in on John Henry Trapp, his horse stepped on a stone and bruised its hoof. Now he was camped out in the middle of nowhere with very few options. He could stay where he was and wait for the damned thing to heal, or he could start walking toward Fort McAdams.

He was furious at the horse for stepping on a stone he could have just as easily missed.

He was furious at Sam Train for hiring him in the first place.

He was furious at John Henry Trapp for not dying in prison.

He was furious at himself for not being able to turn down the job, and for having his own code of ethics. When he took a job he never let anything keep him from doing it—even if it meant walking a full day to get to Fort McAdams.

As far as his options were concerned, if some Comanches happened to show up, he had one other.

He could die.

He could have ridden the horse until he was dead lame, but he decided against that. If he *did* run into some Indians he could mount up and push the animal until he dropped.

Hopefully that wouldn't happen until they reached the safety of the fort.

Angrily he kicked out his campfire and packed his supplies.

Somebody was going to pay for this, and when he caught up to him, that someone would be John Henry Trapp.

Who else was there he could take it out on?

"What is it, Oliver?" Sam Train asked.

The butler eased into the bedroom and moved to Train's bedside.

"I didn't want to wake you, sir," Oliver said.

"How could you wake me?" Train asked. "I'm never asleep. I *can't* sleep anymore. What is it?"

"We just had a visit from a policeman," Oliver said. "He was sent by the chief of police."

"So?"

"It seems the police had an inquiry about you, sir."

"And?"

"Someone wanted to know if you were still . . . er, alive."

Sam Train snorted.

"If you call this living. Who wanted to know?"

"The request came from a man named Fry, from Fort McAdams, in Texas."

"And?"

"The Denver Police routed the reply to the sheriff

of Fort McAdams, and asked him to check it out."

Train closed his eyes and for a moment Oliver thought he had fallen asleep . . . or . . .

"Am I going to have to drag this out of you, Oliver?"

"No, sir," Oliver said. "When the sheriff replied, he mentioned two names. He said he had questioned Fry . . . and Trapp."

"Trapp!" Train said. His reaction was so violent that he began to cough.

"Sir—"

"I'm all right, damn it. Have we heard from Keller?"

"No, sir."

"Well, when we do, tell him that Trapp was asking about me. Now that Trapp knows I'm alive, he'll probably assume that I've sent someone after him. Keller should know that."

"Yes, sir."

"Damn the man!" Train said. "I wish I could see him myself when Keller kills him. I wish I could see it with my own eyes."

"You know that's impossible, sir."

"I know it, you jackass!" Train said. "I just hope I'm still alive when it happens, so I can hear about it. Now, get me out of this damned bed!"

TWENTY-EIGHT

Trapp and Fry debated leaving immediately—now that they had their answer—or waiting until morning.

"Neither one of us is an Indian fighter," Fry said. "I don't mind admitting I don't know when we'd have a better chance of getting by Quanah, now or in the morning."

"Maybe we should find someone to ask," Trapp said.

"That's not a bad idea, Trapp."

They went to the saloon and found the same bartender on duty. They ordered a beer each, and when he set their drinks down in front of them, they asked if he had a minute.

"Sure," he said, wiping his hands on a rag. "What can I do for you?"

"We need to speak to someone who has experience with the Indians."

"What kind of experience?" the man asked. "Living with them? Fighting them?"

"Fighting them, I guess."

"Ah, but a man who lived with them, he'd know them even better."

"Well, who would you suggest?"

"If you want to talk to someone who's lived with them, talk to Jerry Blake. If you want to talk to someone who's fought them, go and see Sergeant Caleb Nichols, at the fort."

Fry looked at Trapp and said, "I guess it wouldn't do any harm to see both of them."

"Why don't you talk to Blake, and I'll go and see Sergeant Nichols."

"All right," Fry said. "I'll meet you back here."

"Right."

Trapp drained his beer, and left the saloon.

"So tell me," Fry said, "where I can find Jerry Blake. . . ."

Trapp went to the fort and asked a soldier where he could find Sergeant Caleb Nichols.

"He's out on patrol right now," Private Rufus McKay replied. "Is this something personal?"

"Well, I understand he's had some experience fighting Indians."

"Oh, yes sir, he sure has—years of it. He's the most experienced Indian fighter in the outfit."

"Do you know when he'll be back?"

"He'll be back in time for mess," McKay said. "I can tell him you was asking for him."

"I'd appreciate it," Trapp said. "Tell him if he

comes over to the saloon, John Trapp would like to buy him a drink."

"I can safely say he'll be there, sir," McKay said. "Ol' Caleb ain't one to turn down a free drink."

Trapp nodded and said, "Thanks for your help."

The one thing the bartender had not told Fry was that Jerry Blake, as well as being a man who had lived with the Indians, was also Fort McAdams's town drunk.

Fry found Blake passed out in the livery. He shook him a few times but it was to no avail. The man did not stir. Fry knew a surefire way to wake up a drunk, and he decided to use it.

He grabbed Blake, a frail man who weighed hardly anything, by the back of the shirt and the back of the belt, and carried him out behind the livery to a horse trough. Once there he unceremoniously dropped the man into the water.

Blake sank like a stone and for a moment Fry thought he wouldn't surface, but finally there he was, sputtering and coughing.

"What the hell—" Blake shouted. He sat up straight, looked around, wiped his face with his hand, then smelled the hand. "It's water!" he said, sounding alarmed.

"It sure is, Blake," Fry said.

"How did I get here?"

"I dropped you in."

"What in the sam hill for?"

"To wake you up."

"Why?"

"To talk to you."

"You woke me to talk?" Blake demanded. "Jesus, if you woke me, the least you could do is buy me a drink."

"Maybe after we talk."

A crafty look came into the water-logged man's eye and he said, "I talk better with one under my belt."

"I don't think you've *ever* had *one* under your belt in your life, Blake," Fry said. "Let's get you out of that water before you catch your death of cold, and we'll see if we can come to some kind of an arrangement."

Fry gave the man his hand and hauled him out of the water.

When Trapp returned to the saloon, he saw Fry sitting at a back table—back to the wall, as always—sitting across from a man who was soaking wet from head to toe. The man didn't seem to mind, though, because Fry was dangling a glass of whiskey in front of him.

"Is this Jerry Blake?" Trapp asked, approaching the table.

"This is Jerry Blake," Fry said. "He's agreed to talk to us, for a price."

"And that price is?" Trapp asked, sitting down.

"A drink."

Trapp eyed the man and asked, "How the hell did he get so wet?"

"That's a long story," Fry said. "Let's just say he took some persuading."

"Can I have—" Blake said, reaching for the drink.

"No, Jerry," Fry said, pulling the drink away, "remember what our deal was. You can smell, but you can't touch."

"Jesus," Blake said, and he put his hands down at his sides.

Fry passed the shot glass beneath the man's nose and Blake breathed in deeply.

"All right," Fry said, removing the glass, "what we want to know is this: We have to leave town and we'd like to avoid meeting up with any of Quanah Parker's boys. How do we do that, by leaving tonight, or in the morning?"

"Is that what this is about?"

"That's it."

Blake looked at the drink mournfully and asked, "Do I still get the drink if you don't like the answer?"

"As long as you *do* answer, you get the drink," Fry said.

"Then you're shit out of luck," Blake said, "because you ain't gonna get by Quanah either way."

"Why not?"

"Because Quanah sees everybody who goes into this fort, and who comes out. He ain't gonna let you two get through, not without trying to stop you."

"Why not?"

"It just ain't his way," Blake said. "Quanah regards this as his land. He ain't just gonna let the white man come and go as he pleases—especially two white men comin' from this fort."

"What do we do then?"

"When you leave you ride like the devil's on your tail—'cause he's gonna be."

177

Trapp and Fry exchanged glances.

"See, I knew you wasn't going to like the answer. Can I have the drink now?"

Without looking at Blake, Fry held the drink out. Blake grabbed it without spilling a drop and drank it down in one swift motion.

"This is not encouraging at all," Fry said. "What did the sergeant have to say?"

"He's out on patrol," Trapp said. "I left a message that there's a free drink waiting for him here."

"We'll just have to wait for him, then, and see what he has to say."

"Uh, how about another?" Blake asked, smacking his lips.

"Here," Trapp said, putting the price of a drink on the table. "Go and buy it yourself."

"You're a good man," Blake said, grabbing the money. "A very good man."

Blake got up and wandered over to the bar.

"What do we do in the meantime?" Trapp said.

Fry looked around. The place was filling up, and he knew that sooner or later a poker game would start up. He didn't mention it to Trapp, though. The memory of what happened the last time he played poker would be too fresh in the old mountain man's mind.

Keller knew they were there.

There were about three or four braves stalking him from behind. He wasn't spooked enough, yet, to mount up and ride. In fact, he might never get that spooked, because so far they had made no move to close the gap between them. It was possible they were just going to watch him, playing some sort of cat-and-mouse game. He knew that if he displayed no fear, the game would go on longer.

Maybe long enough for him to get where he was going—alive!

"Was I you," Sergeant Caleb Nichols said, "I'd leave tonight."

Trapp and Fry had sat together in the saloon for hours waiting for Caleb Nichols to show up, and when he did, they knew him immediately. Apparently, the sergeant had come as soon as he'd returned from patrol, without even cleaning up. He was covered with dust and dirt from head to toe, and had a thirsty look on his face.

Sergeant Caleb Nichols was in his late forties, with a huge belly that hung down over his belt. He was badly in need of a shave and a haircut, but Fry suspected he always looked like that. If he really did have the experience they'd heard about, he probably got away with a lot of things other soldiers wouldn't.

"There some fellas in here who promised me a free drink?" he asked, addressing the entire room.

Fry hesitantly raised his hand. Nichols moved toward them quickly and stared down at both of them eagerly.

"I'm here to collect."

They got the sergeant to sit down, fixed him up with a beer, then put their question to him.

"Why tonight?" Fry asked. "Because Indians don't fight at night?"

"That's a crock of shit," Nichols said. He took a

quick drink, spilling some on the front of his dusty uniform. "Naw, I'd leave tonight because Quanah will think you're two crazy white men, traveling in the dark. He'll probably leave you alone."

Trapp and Fry exchanged a glance.

"You mind traveling at night?" Fry said.

"I just want to get going," Trapp said, "and if we have a better chance at night, let's get moving."

They both stood up and the sergeant said, "Hey, where you going?"

"Thanks for the information, Sarge," Fry said, patting the man on the back. A dust cloud leaped up and spread out, causing Fry to lean away.

"We'll pay for two more beers on the way out, Sergeant Nichols," Trapp said. "You've earned them."

"Well, all right—" Nichols said, but Trapp and Fry were out the door already and on their way to the hotel to get their gear.

TWENTY-NINE

Keller walked into Fort McAdams at first light, looking as if he'd been dragged all the way.

"Looks like you had a rough trip," a soldier said to him.

Keller ignored him and continued to walk, his horse trailing behind him. He walked through the fort and out the rear gate, then asked someone where the livery was. When he had directions, he walked his horse over there.

"He's got a stone bruise," Keller said to the man. "I'll need another mount."

"You can wait three or four days and this here one will heal up," the man said. "He's a good horse."

"I'll need another horse," Keller said. "I'll trade with you."

"If that's what you want," the liveryman said with a shrug.

"Where's the hotel?"

181

"You passed it on the way here," the man said.

"I must have missed it," Keller said.

"Uh, just go back two blocks. It's on the right."

"I'll be back later today for that horse."

"You staying the night?"

"I doubt it," Keller said, and left.

When he got to the hotel, he signed the register. Four names above his he saw the name "Trapp."

"Is this man still here?" he asked the clerk.

The man had to turn the book around to read it.

"Oh, him. Big fella, he was. Came in here filthy as you and walked out clean, with new clothes."

"He left?"

The man nodded.

"Last night, him and his friend."

"Who's his friend?"

"He didn't sign in," the clerk said. "The big fella asked for two rooms."

"You don't know the other man's name?"

"No."

"Would anyone in town know it?"

"Sure," the clerk said, "the sheriff. Those two fellas were involved with a killing."

"I see," Keller said. "I'll be needing a bathtub."

"Down the hall behind me."

Keller nodded and accepted his key.

He took a quick bath, changed into some clean clothes, then went looking for the sheriff.

"Sure I remember those two," Sheriff Keeper said. "Couldn't rightly forget them. One of them, Trapp, was a big fella, although he looked kind of sickly, like he'd lost some weight recently."

"And the other one?" Keller said. "Do you recall his name?"

"Sure," Kepper said. "Fry, Kid Fry. He's got himself a little reputation. It was him the three yahoos were after in the saloon. He got two of them and the other fella, Trapp, got the other one with his buffalo gun. Nearly cut him in half, too."

"I've heard of Fry," Keller said. He was already composing his telegram to Sam Train, telling him that there was an "extra consideration."

"About this big fella, Trapp?" he went on.

"Yeah?"

"Kind of on the old side, isn't he?"

"I suppose so," Keeper said, "but you wouldn't know it to watch him move. Witnesses in the saloon say he moved pretty quick to gun that fella down. He and his friend have a history, too, a recent one. They were involved in killings in Littlesworth and Portsville."

Keller had been in Littlesworth and heard about the shooting there. No one had given him Fry's name then. He had bypassed Portsville, so this was the first he was hearing about the shooting there.

"Those two seem to attract trouble," Keller said.

Keeper laughed.

"That's what I told them when I asked them to leave."

"And did they?"

"What?"

"Did they leave when you asked them?"

"No," Keeper said, "funny thing about that." He went on to tell Keller about the telegrams to and from Denver about a Mr. Sam Train.

"You ever hear of this fella Train?" the lawman asked.

"No," Keller said, standing up, "never."

"Tell me something," Keeper said from his seat behind his desk.

"What?"

"Why are you so interested in those two? Bounty hunter?"

"You guessed."

"I've been a lawman a long time," Keeper said. "You get so you can smell bounty hunters."

Keller knew the man was trying to insult him, but he let it slide. He didn't need trouble with the law at this point.

As he left the sheriff's office, he changed the address of his mental telegram from Sam Train to a "Mr. Oliver."

"Yes, Oliver?"

Sam Train was sitting in his "hot room," thinking about times past when Oliver entered.

"We've heard from Keller."

"Where is he?"

"In Fort McAdams."

"Did he get him?"

"No," Oliver said. "Trapp and Fry were gone when he got there, but it seems this Fry has something of a reputation as a gunman."

"Keller wants more money."

"Under the circumstances," Oliver said, "he thinks it's fair."

"Actually," Train said, "it is. Wire him back and tell him he can have another ten thousand. That should satisfy him, don't you think?"

"I'm sure it will, sir."

"When you come back, Oliver, come in here and smoke a cigar, will you?" Train said. "I feel like smelling some cigar smoke."

"Yes, sir," Oliver said.

Keller left the telegraph office, pocketing the reply from Oliver. The extra ten thousand would be wired to him when he gave them an address. He'd do that as soon as he got to a decent-sized town, with a real bank.

He went to the hotel and checked out.

"But you just checked in," the clerk said.

"So charge me for a half day."

Nervously, the clerk explained he couldn't do that, and Keller didn't argue.

He went to the livery and asked the man if he had a horse picked out for him.

"You want me to pick one out?" the man asked.

"Sure," Keller said, "I trust you, because if I have any problems, I'll be back."

"Er, come with me," the man said nervously.

Keller followed him to a corral in the back.

"That dun's a good horse," the man said.

Keller eyed the animal and decided that it would be a fair trade for his roan.

"All right," he said, "put my rig on him and bring him around front."

"Now? You're leaving now?"

"That's right," Keller said, "I'm leaving now."

While the horse was being saddled, he went to the general store for some supplies. He bought some coffee and bacon, and some dried beef. He figured that Trapp, being from the mountains, would be traveling light, so he wanted to do the same to keep pace.

When he got back to the livery, the dun was saddled and ready.

"You won't have any problems with this animal, mister," the liveryman promised him.

"I hope not," Keller said, mounting up. "For your sake."

The liveryman swallowed heavily.

Keller turned his mount so that he was facing the man.

"Two men left here last night. Were you here?"

"Sure was," the man replied. "They woke me up to open the doors."

"Did they say where they were going?"

"No," the man said, "only that they weren't looking forward to trying to outrun Quanah Parker."

"Quanah won't bother us," Keller said. "We're not carrying anything he wants."

Keller had been stalked all the way to the fort, but since he was walking, it had to be clear to the Indians that he didn't even have a decent horse for them to steal. They had left him alone.

He hoped they would continue to do so.

BOOK FIVE

ORDEAL

THIRTY

Trapp and Fry rode all night without incident. They were not attacked by any Indians; their horses did not step into any chuckholes. As first light dawned, they decided to stop and give the horses a much-deserved rest.

They dismounted and broke out some dried beef for breakfast. They did not want to take the chance of making a camp and relaxing.

"I don't see anything," Fry said, staring out at the flat land around them. "Could they be out there and we don't see them?"

"I suppose so," Trapp said. "In the mountains there are more places to hide. I'm not used to land this flat, this . . . barren."

"When I look at this," Fry said, indicating the flatness around them, "I can't wait to get to your mountain."

"Well, finish your breakfast and we'll get under way," Trapp said.

They chewed the dried beef without enthusiasm, both of them squatting down for comfort. When they rose and reached for their horses, they both saw them at the same time.

"Where the hell did they—" Fry started.

"It doesn't matter," Trapp said. "They're there."

Ahead of them, sitting astride their horses and watching them, were at least a dozen Indian braves. They could only assume that they were Comanches, and that they were Quanah Parker's men.

"Mount up," Trapp said.

Once they were mounted, Fry said, "Should we turn around and make a run for the fort?"

"We'd never make it," Trapp said. "Let's ride straight for them."

"What?"

"Right up to them."

"Are you crazy?"

"No, I'm scared. Are you?"

"You're damned right I am."

"Well, we can't let them see that," Trapp said. "If they even think we're scared, we're dead."

"I thought you didn't know anything about Comanches," Fry said.

"I don't, but I have dealt with Indians."

"Mountain Indians, not plains Indians," Fry said. "They're different."

"There must be some similarities," Trapp said. "They must all respect courage."

"I hope so," Fry said. "If they kill us on the spot, I am going to be very disappointed in you."

"I'll keep that in mind," Trapp said. "Let's go."

They kicked their horses' ribs and started forward. The twelve braves did not move as the two white men approached them.

It seemed to take forever to close the gap between them, but finally they were there and had to rein their horses in. Trapp had a secret hope that they would simply move out of the way and let them pass, but it didn't happen that way.

He studied each of the braves and none of them had blue eyes, so Quanah was not among them.

"Do any of you speak English?" Trapp asked, preferring to make the first move.

All twelve of the braves stared at him.

"Maybe we should try and take them," Fry said.

"No," Trapp said, "some of them have rifles."

"A wise decision," one of the braves said. He was sitting his horse right across from Trapp.

Trapp and Fry looked at each other, then at the brave who had spoken.

"I have never seen a rifle such as that one," the brave said, looking at Trapp's Sharps.

"It is very old," Trapp said.

The brave stared at it a little longer, then looked at them both.

"You will come with us."

"Do we have a choice?" Fry asked.

The brave did not answer.

"I guess we don't," Fry said.

The other braves moved now and in seconds had formed a ring around Trapp and Fry. When the braves started moving, Trapp and Fry had no choice but to move with them.

"They haven't even taken our guns," Fry said, leaning over and speaking softly to Trapp.

"I don't think they feel a need to, Kid," Trapp said. "Do you feel a need to prove them wrong?"

"Not me," Fry said.

"Well then, I guess we're about to get an education of sorts," Trapp said. "Let's sit up straight and pay attention, and maybe we'll get out of this alive."

They rode for a couple of hours and none of the braves ever spoke to them or even looked at them. They were hopelessly penned in by the Indians, so they simply rode along, keeping pace and never trying to slack off.

Finally, they spotted some movement ahead of them. As they drew closer, they saw that it was a village of teepees and fires and people—men, women, and children.

As they rode into the village, they became the center of attention. Children came running up for a closer look, and the circle around them broke to allow it.

Trapp looked down at their open, curious, often dirty faces and wondered suddenly why white men did not think of Indians as people. These were children—*real* children—with a child's curiosity and needs.

He reached down and chucked one black-eyed little boy under the chin. Most of the children were looking at Trapp because they had never seen anyone of his size. Astride his horse he looked like a giant to them.

"They are curious," the lead brave said, looking back at Trapp.

"That's okay," Trapp said. "I don't mind being stared at."

The brave dismounted, and Trapp and Fry followed as the others did the same thing. The little boy Trapp had chucked beneath the chin came running up, then stopped and stared up at him and said something Trapp couldn't understand.

Trapp looked at the brave and asked, "What did he say?"

"He said that you are a giant, even when you are not on a horse."

Trapp towered above everyone in the village. The brave he was speaking to was a half a foot shorter, but he was built along strong lines with a deep chest and thick thighs. Trapp would not have liked to face him in hand-to-hand combat, even thirty years ago.

The boy was still looking up at him with wide eyes so Trapp reached down, took the boy beneath the arms, and lifted him up on his shoulders. The boy shouted, but the smile on his face made it clear that he was not afraid.

"What did he shout?" he asked.

"He said that he is a giant, too," the brave said.

"I hope his father doesn't mind this," Trapp said.

"No," the brave said solemnly, "I do not."

Quanah Parker came out of his teepee to greet his "guests."

He saw two white men walking toward him with Strong Hawk. One of them was very tall and was carrying Strong Hawk's son on his shoulders. Both white men still had their weapons, which indicated that they had not tried to resist when they were taken.

If they had, they would be dead.

Trapp saw the man who had stepped from the teepee. He was tall, not as tall as Trapp, but he would not be as dwarfed by the mountain man as others were.

The boy sat quietly on his shoulders, totally relaxed. Fry walked beside him, anything but relaxed. Trapp hoped that the Kid would be able to hold up and would not make any foolish move.

As for himself, he found that he was curiously at ease in this camp. Certainly more at ease than he had been in any of the white men's towns he'd visited since being released.

As they came closer to the man, Trapp could see clearly that he had blue eyes.

This was Quanah Parker.

THIRTY-ONE

"Why are we here?" Trapp asked.

He and Fry were seated inside Quanah's teepee. The only other person there was the brave who had brought them there. His name, they discovered, was Strong Hawk.

"Strong Hawk brought you here," Quanah said in almost perfect English.

"I know that," Trapp said. "I mean, why did Strong Hawk bring us here?"

"Would you rather he had killed you right away?"

"No," Trapp said, "but I am still curious."

"He watched you ride all night," Quanah said, "and he thought you were"—he groped for the word, then found it—"crazy white men."

"I see."

"He was also *curious*," Quanah Parker said. "He wanted to see what manner of men traveled at night."

"Careful men," Fry said.

Quanah looked at Fry, because these were the first words he had heard the younger man speak.

Quanah himself was in his early thirties, an impressive figure of a man with broad shoulders and powerful arms and legs.

"This is your son?" he asked Trapp.

"No," Trapp said, "my partner."

"Partner?"

"We ride together."

"He is very much younger than you are."

"Yes," Trapp said, "he is."

"It is odd for two such as you to be . . . partners, is it not?"

"Some people might think so."

Quanah looked at Strong Hawk and said something, and the other brave replied.

"What did you say?" Trapp asked.

Quanah looked at him sharply. Trapp guessed that he wasn't used to being questioned.

"I asked him what he wanted to do with you."

"And he said?"

"He did not know," Quanah said. "He has not decided yet."

"Is that for him to decide, or you?" Trapp asked.

"He brought you here," Quanah said. "It is for him to decide."

Quanah stood up.

"Strong Hawk will show you to your teepee."

Trapp and Fry stood up.

"Before you leave," Quanah said, "leave your weapons there." He pointed to a blanket lying on the floor.

This is it, Trapp thought. Fry might think that he had a chance in here, with only two of them, to do some damage. Trapp had to head him off.

Before Trapp could say anything, though, Fry said, "Sure, why not? After all, we're your guests, right? What do we need guns for?"

Fry unbuckled his gun and dropped it on the blanket. Trapp laid his Sharps down next to it.

"Go with Strong Hawk," Quanah said, and turned his back.

Strong Hawk stepped outside and they followed.

"Nice move, Kid," Trapp said.

"What did you think I was going to do?" Fry asked. "Draw on them? We'd still have the rest of this village to deal with."

"We're just going to have to wait and see what they have in mind for us," Trapp said.

"What *he* has in mind for us," Fry said, pointing ahead of them to Strong Hawk.

"Quanah seems to be a leader who doesn't mind letting his people think for themselves."

"I just wish we knew what this one was thinking."

"Maybe we should just ask him," Trapp suggested.

"Do you think he'd tell us?"

"No."

"Do you think he'd take our asking as a sign of weakness?"

"Probably."

"Then maybe we shouldn't ask," Fry said.

"Maybe you're right."

Strong Hawk stopped at a teepee and said, "This is yours."

"Mine?" Trapp asked.

"Both of you."

Fry looked at Trapp and said, "Ours."

"Right."

"Quanah says you are our guests," Strong Hawk said.

"And we want to thank him—" Trapp began, but Strong Hawk wasn't listening.

"Do not try to escape," he said, and turned and walked away.

Trapp and Fry looked around and noticed that there were several braves watching them.

"So much for being guests," Trapp said.

"Yeah."

"Come on, let's get out of the sun."

They went inside the teepee, which was not as large as Quanah Parker's. There were a couple of blankets on the ground, but they weren't needed at the moment.

They each picked out a place on the floor and sat down.

"I don't know how we're ever going to get to my mountain if we can't even get out of Texas," Trapp said glumly.

"Well, there ain't much we can do about it now," Fry said. "We're in Quanah's hands."

"Maybe we can escape."

"Without our guns and horses? You think this land is flat now, wait until you try to walk it."

Trapp's shoulders slumped and he said, "I'll take your word for it."

* * *

Keller knew there wasn't much chance of tracking Trapp and Fry through the hard plains. There was a scuff mark here and a cold campfire there, but much of the time he simply traveled in a straight line, hoping he was going in the right direction.

There was something else he used, though, and it was something he had developed over years of hunting men. It was called *instinct*.

His instinct was attuned to John Henry Trapp, and he *knew* that he was heading in the right direction. It also helped to know that Trapp was a mountain man, and was surely heading back to the mountains. Even if Keller was *not* on Trapp's trail, they would both end up in the same place.

The Rockies.

According to the information he'd gotten from Oliver, Sam Train's butler, Trapp came from the Green River country of the Central Rockies.

He would continue to travel in a straight line until he reached there.

Hopefully, he'd get to Oklahoma without running into any of Quanah's Comanches.

That hope was dashed quickly enough.

He was walking his horse, resting it without stopping, studying the ground. When he looked up, there was suddenly a row of Comanches in front of him. At least he *assumed* they were Comanches.

He reined his horse in and watched them, but all they did was watch him. He correctly guessed that they were waiting for him to run. If he did, they would probably ride him down and kill him.

He took his pistol from his holster and very deliberately dropped it to the ground, then followed with his rifle.

They approached him and formed a circle around him, and one brave retrieved his weapons. After that, they herded him to their camp.

He had made the right decision, and he was alive—for now.

"Sounds like some commotion outside," Trapp said.

Fry had heard it also. They both rose and moved to look outside. It was the first sound of activity in the hours they had been there, other than the one time an Indian girl had come to them with some food.

"What are we eating?" Fry had asked, chewing some of the stringy meat.

"I may be wrong," Trapp said, "but I think it's dog."

"Dog?"

"Tastes like some wolf meat I once had."

Fry had stared at the meat for a few moments, then shrugged and said, "What the hell," and continued eating.

Now Trapp said, "Looks like we're going to have some company."

"Know him?" Fry asked, then said, "No, of course, you wouldn't. You've only been out a matter of weeks."

"I take it you don't know him?"

"No, I've never seen him before."

"Looks like he made the right decision, too," Trapp said.

"I guess Strong Hawk is going to have another decision to make."

"I wonder what he was doing out there all alone."

"Maybe he wasn't alone," Fry said. "Maybe the people he was with didn't make the right decision, like he did."

"I guess we'll find out," Trapp said. "They're bringing him over here."

"Gonna bunk him in with us, huh?" Fry said. "They don't have real private accommodations around here, do they?"

They backed away from the entrance as the man and his escort reached the teepee. The flap was thrown back and the man entered. He stood up straight and stared at Trapp and Fry.

"Do you two know what's going on here?" he asked.

"Apparently," Fry said, "we are the reluctant guests of Quanah Parker."

"Ah, so they *are* his men."

"Yeah," Fry said, "we've seen him."

The man studied them both for a moment, and Trapp had the impression that he was being measured for . . . something.

"My name is Flynn," the man finally said. "Douglas Flynn."

"How do you do, Mr. Flynn," Trapp said. "I'm John Trapp."

Trapp shook hands with the man and was impressed by the confidence of the grip. The man was powerful, but felt no need to prove it. That indicated a confident man.

201

"Fry," Fry said, shaking hands briefly.

"How long have you fellas been here?" the man asked.

"Just a few hours longer than you have," Fry said, although it was more like six or seven hours. "They took us this morning."

"Without a fight?"

"We were slightly outnumbered," Trapp said.

"Yes, so was I," the man said. "Was it just the two of you?"

"Yes," Trapp said, "just us two."

The man nodded.

"Yeah, I was alone," the man said. He rubbed his hands together and looked around at their somewhat cramped quarters.

"Well, what are we supposed to do now?"

"I guess we just wait," Trapp said, "and see what they have in mind for us."

"I suppose they intend to kill us," the man said. "They're just deciding whether to do it slow or quick."

"That's a possibility," Trapp said. "My guess is they intend to test us."

"Test us?"

Trapp nodded.

"Test our courage."

"Well," the man said, "I hope we're all up to it."

Yeah, Trapp thought to himself, so do I.

Keller couldn't believe his mixed luck. He'd been captured by the Comanches, and then thrown in together with the very men he'd been hunting. Standing in front of him was thirty-five thousand dollars, twenty-five of which he had already collected.

He still intended to earn that money, and he had no intention of letting the extra ten thousand get away.

All he had to do was figure out a way for the three of them to get away alive, so he could kill both of them.

The night passed without incident.

No one came to take any of them away, and no one came to bring them any more food. They gave what they had left to the new man, Flynn.

"This tastes like dog," he said, after taking a nibble.

"That's what I thought," Trapp said. "You've eaten it before?"

"Mr. Trapp, I've eaten almost everything there is to eat," Flynn/Keller said. "Dog, mule, snake, rat—"

"You sound like you've had a rather . . . interesting life," Trapp said.

To Trapp, Flynn looked to be in his forties. He was a healthy specimen, so he hadn't had to eat any of those things lately.

Fry noticed that the man called Flynn's holster was well worn, but also well cared for.

When they had a chance, they could compare notes about him.

Just before they decided to turn in, someone did come along, but it was only a man's arm poking in and dropping another blanket on the floor.

"Kind of them," Keller said, picking up the blanket.

"They don't want us to freeze to death," Fry said, "but they don't want to feed us too much, to keep our strength up."

"I think we'd better get a good night's rest," Trapp

said. "Whatever they have in store for us, we're going to have to be ready."

"I agree," Keller said.

Fry nodded and they all lay down and made themselves as comfortable as possible.

In the morning they were awakened abruptly. Five braves rushed into the teepee and hauled them to their feet without warning. They were pushed outside, where they all stood shielding their eyes from the bright sun.

"What the hell is going on?" Fry demanded, but no one was answering.

Suddenly, they were seized again, this time from behind, and their shirts were stripped off.

"This is not looking good," Keller said.

Next they were lifted off their feet and their boots were removed.

"This is definitely looking bad," Fry said.

"If they try to take my pants, I'm leaving," Keller said.

Trapp thought that the humor on both their parts sounded a bit forced. He also hoped that their nerve would hold up, no matter what they had in front of them.

Trapp considered that he was probably calmer because, being a lot older than the Kid and Flynn, he had less to lose. Maybe being sixty-four was finally going to work in his favor.

Finally, Quanah stepped out of his teepee, but he did not approach them. Instead, Strong Hawk came over to talk to them.

"You will have a head start," he said, "and then my braves will hunt you down."

"I don't understand what I'm doing here—" Flynn/Keller began, but Strong Hawk silenced him with a quick look.

"You are being tested," Strong Hawk said, then he smiled thinly and added, "I am interested in seeing how much courage you have."

"Well, I was riding through your land alone, wasn't I?" he asked.

"That could have been foolishness," Strong Hawk said, "even stupidity. Now we will see how truly courageous you are."

"And how sound the soles of our feet are," Fry said. Already the ground beneath his feet was starting to heat up from the sun.

Strong Hawk moved over in front of Trapp and stared at him.

"You are quiet."

"I have nothing to say."

"You interest me most of all," the brave said. "You are older, but are you wiser?"

"I don't believe wisdom is what will get us through this," Trapp said.

"Of the three," Strong Hawk said, "I believe you will survive—if any of you do."

"Him?" Keller asked. "He's an old man. He'll never survive out there. When the sun gets real hot—"

"Silence!" Strong Hawk said. "You are wasting what little time you have."

"What are we supposed to do?" Keller asked.

"Run," Strong Hawk said. "Just . . . run, and keep running until nightfall. Whichever of you returns here after dark will go free."

Keller looked at Fry, who looked at Trapp, who said, "I suggest we start running."

"Here," Strong Hawk said, and handed Trapp a knife.

"What about me?" Keller asked.

"One knife for the three of you," Strong Hawk said. "Go."

"Maybe I better hold the knife, old timer," Keller said.

"Trapp's a mountain man, Flynn," Fry said. "If anyone knows how to handle a knife, he does."

"Let's get moving," Trapp said.

They started running, each with their own stride.

Trapp had a long, loping, easy stride.

Fry's stride was shorter, but no less fluid.

Keller was used to riding, and running had never been a strong point with him. His stride was short and choppy, and of the three he was sure to tire first.

"I wonder why they gave us one knife," Fry said aloud.

"Two reasons that I could think of," Trapp said.

"What . . . are they?" Keller asked. They had run maybe two hundred yards, and he was beginning to labor already.

"First, I think they wanted to see if we would fight over it," Trapp said.

Fry gave Keller a glance, and the man looked away.

"What's the second reason?" Keller asked.

"I think they're hedging their bets," Trapp said. "I think they feel that the one knife will keep the three of us together. That way, we'll only be as fast as the slowest runner, and we'll be easy to find, and catch."

"Then what you're saying is that we should split up," Fry said.

"Exactly."

"Who gets the knife?" Fry asked.

"I do," Keller said.

"Why you?" Fry asked.

"That's easy," Keller said. "I'm the one they're gonna catch first. I mean, already my lungs are burning. Look at Trapp. He's not even breathing hard."

"Yeah," Fry said, "not bad for an old man, huh?"

"All right," Keller said, "I'm sorry for that. Maybe I panicked a little."

"None of us can afford to panic," Trapp said. "If we do, we're dead."

"Hey, who are we kidding?" Keller asked. "We're dead anyway, it's just a matter of when."

Trapp reached across Fry's chest and handed Keller the knife. Keller looked at Fry before taking it.

"Good luck, fellas," Trapp said, and veered off to his left, increasing his pace.

"That guy's unbelievable," Keller said. "How old is he?"

"Sixty-four."

"Living in the mountains must do wonders for you," Keller said. "Jesus . . . I've got to stop and rest."

Fry stopped with him as Keller leaned over to catch his breath. He held the knife in his right hand, and it would have been very easy for him to kill Fry right there and then. All he had to do was bring the knife up into Fry's belly, twist it, and leave him on the ground, gutted.

"We don't have time to rest, Flynn," Fry said. "I'm gonna keep going, and I suggest you do the same."

"Yeah," Keller said, looking up at Fry as he tried in vain to catch his breath. "Yeah . . . sure . . . good luck, Fry."

"Good luck," Fry said. "Maybe we'll all make it back."

THIRTY-TWO

Trapp was surprised.

He had expected to feel tired, but he didn't. In fact, he felt almost invigorated by the simple act of running. It was *pleasure* to be able to run again, after so many years—but he knew it wouldn't last. As the sun got higher and hotter, it would drain his strength. He might last longer than the others, but not as long as he might have twenty-five years ago.

The sun on his neck and back felt hot already, and the ground beneath his feet did as well. Fry would be all right for a while. After all, he was twenty-five years old. It dawned on him that Fry may not have even been born when he himself first went into prison.

The man who called himself Flynn had looked done in almost immediately, and might have already been run down by the fleet-footed Comanches.

Trapp couldn't afford to think about Flynn now, or

even Fry. They were going to have to look after themselves, just as he was.

He didn't know how far he was from the border into Oklahoma, but he doubted he could make it on foot. His only chance was to survive until the sun went down and then return to camp. He'd have to hope that Strong Hawk—and behind him Quanah Parker—were men of their word.

He looked around and noticed for the first time that the plains terrain was not quite flat. There were rises and depressions—surely nothing like the mountains, but not quite as flat as a desert either. He might be able to put those rises and depressions to use. However, surviving would be a lot easier if he had a weapon.

He started to check out the ground as he loped over it. The only thing he was likely to find was a sharp rock, something sharp enough to inflict damage. He wondered briefly what would happen if he killed any of Quanah's braves. Would he still be allowed to go free upon returning to camp?

His feet were starting to burn. He looked around and saw *some* vegetation, but there was nothing he could use to cover his feet, except his pants.

He stopped running and sat down on the hard ground. He tried to tear one of his pant legs, but the jeans were too tough. Quickly he removed the pants and started gnawing at the leg with his teeth. When he'd managed to chew through, he tore it and went to work on the other leg.

Eventually he had enough material to wrap both of his feet. He tore some thinner strips from the pants and used them to tie the cloth around his feet. He then slipped on what was left of his pants. The legs now barely reached his knees.

He stood up and ran a few steps and then stopped to tighten the strips. Satisfied that his feet were protected at least from the heat, he started running again. Of course, the material would not protect his feet from getting cut on something sharp, so he was just going to have to watch his step.

Fry was livid, and the pain brought tears to his eyes.

He had stepped on a sharp piece of rock and cut his foot. He was angry at himself for his clumsiness.

Sitting on the hard ground, he inspected the wound. It wasn't deep, but it was bleeding a lot. He pulled his handkerchief from his pocket and tied it tightly around the wound. He looked behind him and wondered just how much of a head start Strong Hawk had given them. He still could not see any Comanches—but he realized that he *wouldn't* see them if they didn't want to be seen. Maybe they had him well within their sights but were playing with him.

Maybe standing up and running on the cut foot would be a waste of time.

He stood up and tested the foot. It still hurt, but he realized that he couldn't feel the heat of the ground through the handkerchief. If he'd had another one, he could have bound the other foot as well.

He sat down again and tried to tear one of his pant legs. When that didn't work, he took off the pants, tore one leg with his teeth, then continued to tear until he had what he wanted. He did the same thing with the other leg and double wrapped his wounded foot. He did not know that Trapp had done the same thing, but what other way was there for them to protect their feet?

It was easier for Keller to protect his feet. He simply cut the strips he needed from his pants with the knife and then tied them to his feet. He sat where he was longer than was wise, but he had to get his breath back.

He wondered how many braves would be after them, and how they'd split up when they figured out that the three white men had separated.

Would they figure that out? Of the three of them, Fry was the one who had continued on. Trapp had veered off to the left, and Keller to the right.

Maybe they'd have to run Fry down and kill him before they realized the white men had separated. That would give Keller and Trapp more time to survive. Once Fry was dead, it didn't matter who had killed him. Keller could collect the ten thousand dollars anyway.

The thought surprised Keller. In the past he never would have claimed payment for a job he didn't do. Being in this predicament had made him realize how much he wanted to live. With thirty-five thousand dollars, maybe he could retire from manhunting and enjoy the rest of his life.

If he *had* a rest of his life.

Trapp found a rock formation, and it presented him with a dilemma.

It was certainly the kind of thing someone would use for cover, and he *would* have used it if he'd had a gun. The way things stood now, if he tried to hide behind it, the braves would catch up to him. They'd *know* that he was behind it and would have to try and get him out.

What would happen, he wondered, if he managed to survive until dark? If the braves got to him in the dark, would they kill him anyway? Probably. The deal was that he had to *return* to camp in order to survive.

He reached the formation and found it was quite large. It could have easily afforded three men with guns ample cover to hold off a group of Indians.

For him it simply represented a place to die.

Fry wondered how many square miles Texas had. That was something he'd like to find out if they got out of this. He also wished he knew how many miles he had run already. He was sure it wasn't as much as his aching legs were telling him.

Ah, it was probably better if he didn't know.

Keller still couldn't see any of the Comanches. For a moment he wondered if it was all a joke. What if Strong Hawk really didn't send anyone after them at all? What if they were running around out here for no reason?

Keller decided that wasn't the case. He didn't know all that much about Comanches, but he didn't really think they had a sense of humor.

He couldn't see them.

That worried Trapp. If they were on his tail, he should have been able to see them by now.

He stopped running as something occurred to him. He didn't know how well even a Comanche could track over this terrain. Would they know that the three white men had split up? Or would they simply keep running away from their camp—in which case they would eventually run down Fry, or Flynn, whichever had continued to run in a straight line.

Trapp turned around and started running back the way he'd come, but on a diagonal course. He hoped that he would intercept either Fry or Flynn, and he hoped he was right and he wouldn't run headlong into a bunch of Comanches.

Fry could hear them.

They were making sounds like animals on a hunt, and maybe that's what they were. He turned his head and saw them. There were half a dozen of them, and they were all running his way. Was six all Strong Hawk had sent out, or had they split into three groups?

Fry's lungs were burning, and now his feet were burning, even through what was left of the material he'd wrapped his feet in. The cut foot hurt like hell and all he wanted to do was sit down and rest.

If he sat down, he'd get a lot of rest, all right.

He'd rest *forever*.

Keller stopped running and looked back. He couldn't see anyone, and he became convinced that no one was coming—not for him anyway. That meant they were trailing either Trapp or Fry.

Trapp and Fry were white men, just like him. Keller

had never had friends, not in his whole life, but if he had to pick between a red man and a white man, he'd pick the white man every time.

Maybe—just maybe—if they stuck together, they'd get out of this alive.

He turned around and began to run back, but he chose a diagonal course. Maybe he'd cross paths with Fry, and maybe they should then turn and face the Comanches. At least they'd die fighting, and not running.

Keller was nothing if not a fighter.

Trapp looked ahead and wasn't quite sure he was seeing right. Maybe his eyes were playing tricks on him. The heat was coming up from the ground, creating a haze, but it looked to him as though he was running up on about six Comanche braves—and farther ahead of them was the figure of a running man.

It was either Fry or Flynn.

During his run back, Trapp had stopped several times to pick up likely-looking stones, big enough to fit into his hands but not so heavy he couldn't carry them. Now he wanted only to get close enough to the Indians to chuck the stones at them. With a little luck he might be able to knock out one or two of them. That would leave four for him and the other man to handle.

Fighting and dying was a better idea to him than continuing to run and run and run, and then maybe dying anyway.

At least this way he was in control of his own destiny. Sort of.

* * *

Keller stared ahead of him, through the heat haze that was drifting up from the ground. Was he seeing right? It looked as if there were six Indians ahead of him.

His right hand tightened on the knife and he wondered if he could close on them and dispatch at least one before they saw or heard him.

How good was a Comanche's hearing anyway?

Fry turned and looked over his shoulder once again. They were closing on him. A few hundred yards more and they'd be on him, and he'd probably be too tired to fight them.

He stopped running abruptly and turned around.

"Come on, you ornery redskins, come and get it!" he shouted—at least, he'd intended to shout. What came out of his dry mouth could not have even been called a whisper.

Damn, and all he had gotten for the effort was cracked lips.

Trapp saw Fry stop running. For a moment he thought his friend was giving up, but from the way Fry was gesticulating at the Indians, that was the farthest thing from his mind.

At the same time he saw Flynn coming from the other direction, brandishing the knife in his right hand.

Great minds, he thought.

He wondered which of them the Comanches would notice first, himself or Flynn.

By some wild coincidence they were all coming together at the same place at the same time.

He wondered what the final outcome would be, and let fly with a rock.

THIRTY-THREE

The stone struck one of the Indians on the head, knocking him down, and maybe even out—but that was not all it accomplished.

As the Indian fell, a couple of his cronies turned their heads to see where the stone had come from. Naturally, they saw Trapp running toward them and shouted to the rest of their friends.

They were now aware of Fry ahead of them, waving his arms and trying in vain to shout, and Trapp behind them, chucking the rest of his stones.

They were sufficiently distracted by both men that they never saw Flynn/Keller until it was too late. He was on them, hacking at them with his knife.

Fry, seeing what was happening, stopped waiting for the Indians to reach him and ran forward.

Trapp, stoneless now, reached the group and picked up the knife that belonged to the Indian he'd stoned. Everything that came after that was instinct.

He stepped forward, took hold of one brave's chin from behind, and pulled his head back. He brought the sharp edge of the knife across his throat, slashing it wide open. As the brave's blood stained the ground, he released him and went on to the next one.

Fry reached the fray and literally threw himself into it without hesitation.

Keller, on the ground with two Indians, slid his knife between the ribs of one of them and lashed out at the other with his elbow.

Trapp slid his arm around the throat of another brave, grasped his chin with the other hand, and broke the red man's neck.

Fry fronted the last standing Indian and hit him as hard as he could in the face with his fist.

The last conscious Indian was the other one on the ground, struggling with Keller, whose knife had somehow become wedged in the body of the Indian he'd stabbed. The second Indian he was struggling with raised his knife and started to stab downward. The arc of his knife was intercepted by Trapp's hand, which clamped down on his wrist.

Fry came over, pulled the knife from the Indian's hand, and drove it down into the back of the man's neck. The Indian shuddered once, then fell still, his dead weight pinning Keller to the ground. Trapp and Fry pulled him off and assisted the man they knew as Flynn to his feet.

"What took you guys so long?" Fry asked.

After checking all the bodies, Trapp said, "Four dead and two knocked out."

"We can fix that easy enough," Keller said. He leaned down to slit the throat of one of the unconscious Indians, but Trapp's big hand stopped him.

"What's wrong?" Keller asked. "You want them to get up and come after us again?"

"We don't have to kill them."

"Trapp," Fry said, "I think I have to agree with Flynn here. We don't even know if these six are all Strong Hawk sent out. There may be more. We have to make sure these two don't get up and come after us again."

Trapp was still dubious, but he realized that they had already killed four of Quanah's men. If the Comanche leader was going to kill them for that, they wouldn't be any more dead for killing two more.

"Shit," Trapp said, but he released Flynn/Keller's hand.

While Keller slit the throat of one, Fry leaned over and took care of the other one.

"You fellas better take a pair of moccasins each," Trapp said. "We still have a long time to spend out here."

"What about you?" Fry asked, removing the footwear of one brave and trying them on.

"None of these fellas had feet my size," Trapp said.

"These fit," Flynn/Keller said happily.

Fry also found a pair that fit, and stood up.

"Let's take their knives," Trapp said. He picked up two and stuck them in his belt, and the others followed. They now had seven knives between them.

"We're going to have to assume that there are other Comanches out there looking for us," Fry said.

Trapp looked up at the sun and said, "We've still

got a good five hours left before we can even start thinking about getting back to camp."

"Are your feet going to be all right?" Fry asked Trapp. He hadn't told either of the other men about his cut foot. The moccasins were going to make that a lot easier to handle.

"I'll be fine," Trapp said.

"Considering how well we did here," Keller said, "maybe we should stick together this time."

Trapp and Fry agreed.

"I know a place we can hole up for a while," Trapp said, thinking of that rock formation he'd passed. "We might as well just wait and see what else we're going to have to deal with."

"Does it offer any shade?" Keller asked.

"It does."

"Then lead the way, partner," Fry said.

When they reached the rock formation, they sat on the shady side and kept a sharp eye out for Comanches.

"You know," Fry said, "I'm starting to think we might get out of this alive."

"If Quanah and Strong Hawk are men of their word," Trapp said. "I just hope the death of six braves doesn't outweigh that."

"We didn't have any other choice," Keller said. "I think we all had the same thing in mind."

"To die fighting," Fry said.

"Exactly."

Fry turned to Trapp, but the older man was staring off into space.

"What's he thinking about?" Keller asked.

"His mountain."

"Mountain?"

"The Rocky Mountains," Fry said. "That's where we were headed when we got caught."

"What for?"

"That's where he lives."

"What was he doing all the way out here?"

Fry looked at Keller, whom he knew as Flynn, and said, "It's a long story."

"I've got nothing but time," the other man said.

Fry was about to reply when Trapp said, "You fellas better get some rest. I'll keep watch. If we have to take on the whole Comanche nation when we get back, we'd better be rested."

"Good point," Fry said. He looked at Keller and said, "I'll tell you about it another time."

"If there is another time," Keller said.

"There will be," Trapp said. "I'm not going to let even a bunch of Comanches keep me from getting back to my mountain."

BOOK SIX
SHOWDOWN

THIRTY-FOUR

Fry woke to find Trapp shaking him.

"Horses," Trapp said.

Fry remained still, listening intently. Trapp must have had incredible ears, because he didn't hear a thing. Moments later, he did hear it.

"Wake Flynn," Trapp said.

"I'm awake," Flynn/Keller said, opening his eyes.

They all got up and began to look around.

"They can't be Indian ponies," Trapp said.

"Why not?" Fry asked.

"That would mean that Quanah broke his word."

"Is that so hard to believe?" Keller asked.

"For some reason," Trapp said, "yes."

"Look," Fry said.

Both Trapp and Keller looked in the direction Fry was pointing—the opposite direction from where they might have expected the Indians to come.

"Three riders," Fry said, "and they're white."

"They're soldiers," Trapp said.

All three of them stepped out from the rock formation and began to wave. After a few moments the riders spotted them and changed direction. When they reached the three white men they stared, for they made a strange sight with their tattered clothes, their skin red from the sun, and their lips cracked.

"What the hell are you three doing out here?" one soldier asked. He was wearing sergeant's stripes. The other soldier was a private. The third man was not a soldier, but a civilian scout.

Quickly, Trapp explained their predicament.

"Well, we're riding in advance of a supply train," the sergeant said. "You can ride double with us until we reach the wagons."

"Thanks," Trapp said, "we appreciate it."

"Any sign of Comanches, Jeter?" the sergeant asked the scout.

"No, sir," the man said, pausing to spit tobacco juice, "nary a sign."

"Let's go, then," the sergeant said, "before we run into them."

Trapp got up behind the sergeant while Fry climbed up behind the private, and Keller rode double with the scout.

"I'd say you fellas were pretty damn lucky we came along," the sergeant said to Trapp.

"And I'd say you were right, Sergeant," Trapp said. "Some good luck was just what we needed."

When the supply train reached Fort McAdams, Trapp, Fry, and Keller climbed down from the wagons and again thanked the sergeant, whose name was Casey.

"The major's going to want to talk to all three of you," Casey said. "Your information might finally lead us to Quanah's camp."

"We'll be happy to tell the major all we know, Sergeant, after we clean up a little," Trapp said.

"Surely," the sergeant said. "Just come over to the fort and ask for me, and I'll take you boys over to see him."

The three of them started walking to the rear gate and stopped there.

"Where you headed?" Trapp asked Keller.

"Well, there's a stop I'd like to make even before the hotel," Keller replied, "so I guess I'll be seeing you boys around."

As Keller walked away Fry said, "I wonder what's more important to him than getting cleaned up."

"Maybe he's going to buy some clothes."

"We're going to need some clothes also," Fry said. "We have to have something to change into."

Luckily, while leaving them their pants, Quanah had also left them their money, which was in their pockets.

They walked over to the general store to buy some shirts, jeans, and boots, and thought it odd that they didn't see Flynn there.

After that they went to the hotel and asked the clerk if they could have their rooms back.

"Sure," the clerk said. "Ain't filled them yet."

He turned the register around so they could sign in.

"By the way, did your friend find you?"

"What friend?" Trapp asked.

"Fella who came in here yesterday asking for you," the clerk said. "There's his name, right there."

Trapp looked at Fry and then they both looked at the name on the register.

"Keller," Fry said. "Why does that sound familiar?"

"What did he look like?" Trapp asked.

The clerk described Keller, and both Trapp and Fry realized that he was also describing the man they knew as Flynn.

They backed away from the desk so the clerk couldn't hear them talking.

"What's going on?" Trapp asked.

"Wait a minute," Fry said. "I know a Keller. He's a bounty hunter, a killer for hire."

Trapp rubbed his jaw and said, "He must have been hired by Sam Train."

"But why didn't he kill us out there when he had the chance?" Fry asked.

"Because out there we needed each other to survive," Trapp said. "My guess is buying a gun was more important to him than clothes or a hotel room."

"Good point," Fry said, "and that means we'd better get some guns, and fast."

It was then that Trapp realized that his Sharps was still back in Quanah's camp.

"You take your bath and get changed," Fry said. "I'll go and get a gun."

"You'd better be careful you don't run into him on the street," Trapp said. "Maybe we'd better go together."

"One would be less noticeable than two," Fry said.

"All right," Trapp said, "but why don't you see if this fella here behind the desk has a gun you can borrow, just for now."

They went back to the desk and posed the question to the clerk.

"Well, I do have an old Walker Colt back here," the man said, "but I keep it in case of trouble."

"I'll rent it from you," Trapp said.

"How much?"

"Two dollars, for an hour."

The clerk brought out the gun and handed it over. Trapp gave it to Fry and paid the man.

"Is it loaded?" Trapp asked.

"Yeah, and I think it'll even fire."

Fry tucked the gun into his pants.

"Here," Trapp said, "put on one of these shirts, or you'll attract everyone's attention."

Fry slipped into one of the clean shirts and tucked it in, so it wouldn't lie over the gun.

"I'll be back soon," Fry said.

"Get me a rifle," Trapp said.

"What kind?"

"It doesn't matter," Trapp said. "Something cheap. I just wish I had my Sharps."

"Too bad," Fry said. "It was a beautiful old gun."

Fry left and Trapp turned to the desk man.

"I'll need a bath," he said, "a hot one."

After leaving Trapp and Fry, Keller went directly to the gunsmith's store.

"Well, what happened to you?" the man behind the counter asked.

"I need a gun and a rig."

"You look like you need a bath, a room, and a doctor, not necessarily in that order."

"First a gun," Keller said, staring at the clerk.

"Well, er, sure . . . that's what I'm here for."

Keller felt naked without a gun, now that they were back in civilization. Once he had one, he'd get cleaned up, then he'd take care of Trapp and Fry, and get started on his retirement.

THIRTY-FIVE

Fry walked down the street quickly and as he was approaching the gunsmith shop he saw Keller, looking ragged and beat, step out. For a moment Fry considered bracing him, but the man was wearing a brand new rig on his hip, and all Fry had was the old Walker Colt tucked into his pants. He stepped into a doorway and watched Keller cross the street. When he reached the other side he started walking, but not in the direction of the hotel. Fry waited until Keller had gone a full block, then stepped out of the doorway and made for the gunsmith shop.

Trapp would have liked to soak in the hot tub longer, but he kept thinking that Keller was going to break in on him any minute. He soaped off, washed his hair and beard, then got out of the tub. He changed into his fresh clothes and pulled on his new boots. It felt odd to have boots on again after all the barefoot running he had done that day.

He wondered idly what Quanah Parker would do when he and Fry and Keller did not return that night—and neither did his six braves.

He stepped out into the hall cautiously and walked back to the lobby. As he came out from behind the desk, Fry came walking in, wearing a gun on his hip. The holster looked worn, as did the gun in it.

"Here," Fry said, handing Trapp a rifle. "It's an old Winchester, but the shop wasn't exactly well stocked with new guns. I had to settle for this used Colt, but I took it because it's in good working order. Oh, yeah, here," Fry said, handing the Walker Colt to the desk clerk. "Thanks."

"Any time," the clerk said, putting the gun back beneath the counter.

"Why don't you get a bath and I'll watch for Keller," Trapp said.

"Come on back with me and we'll talk while I wash," Fry said.

They went into the back and Trapp sat in a straightbacked wooden chair by the door while Fry took a considerably more leisurely bath than he had.

"It's getting dark," Fry said. "I wonder what Quanah Parker's going to think."

"He's going to think that the three white men got clean away," Trapp said, "and we did—with a little help."

"When I get out of the bath, let's go and talk to the major. Maybe now that we have valuable information for him, we can get an escort tomorrow."

"First I think we'll have to deal with Keller," Trapp said. "He's probably been on our trail for a while.

That was what he was doing out there alone. Now that we're all here together, I don't think he'll want to let the opportunity pass."

"Maybe he'll wait until tomorrow," Fry said hopefully, "when we've rested up some."

"You know, Fry, there's no reason you have to get involved with Keller—"

"Stop right there," Fry said. "We're partners, remember? Besides, Keller must know all about me by now. My guess is he's made separate arrangements with Train to cover my presence."

"I guess you're right."

"I'm coming out," Fry said, standing up. "I want to talk to that major before it gets much later."

As Fry was drying off, Trapp saw a deep, livid scar on his left buttock, but didn't ask about it right then. There were other things to be settled, first.

Trapp felt odd walking with the Winchester in his hand instead of the Sharps. This gun was so much lighter than the Sharps that he almost felt unbalanced.

They went to the fort and asked for Sergeant Casey. They were asked to wait by the corral while a soldier went to fetch him.

"Well, Trapp and Fry," Casey said, coming up on them. They had exchanged names while riding double. "Where's your friend?"

"Actually, we never saw him before they brought him into Quanah's camp, so we're not friends," Fry said.

"We don't know where he is," Trapp said.

"Well, that doesn't matter," Casey said. "You two

can tell the major everything you know. Come on. He's waiting in his office."

They entered the major's office and Casey spoke to his aide, the young lieutenant who had admitted Trapp and Fry to see the major the first time.

"I'll tell him you're here," the lieutenant said, and went into the major's office.

"That shavetail is a real asshole," Casey said.

The lieutenant came back and said, "The major will see you now."

"No kidding," the sergeant said under his breath. "Come on, gents."

Casey led the way into the major's office.

"These are the men I told you about, Major."

"Well," the major said, recognizing them, "you two again."

"You've met?" Casey asked.

"Oh yes," the major said. "These fellas were interested in getting through the Staked Plains without running into Quanah Parker."

"It doesn't look like they did it, sir."

"If I didn't know better," the major said, "I'd think you fellas got yourself caught so you'd have something to trade. All right, have a seat and let's go over this."

Using a map on the wall, Trapp and Fry related their experience to the major. With the information they gave him, the commanding officer felt that he had finally pinpointed the location of Quanah's camp.

"If this works out, you fellas will be heroes," the major said.

"We'll settle for an escort off these plains," Trapp said.

"You'll have it," the major said. "Casey will be taking some wagons over the plains at the end of the week."

Trapp and Fry looked at each other. If they had to stay here until the end of the week—four more days—Keller would have plenty of time to do what he was hired to do.

"I'll send out a patrol tomorrow," the major said. "In fact, I'll take them out myself. I'm grateful to you men for this information."

"And we're grateful to Sergeant Casey for finding us," Trapp said.

"By tomorrow afternoon we should know something," the major said. "Will you be in the hotel?"

"We will."

"I'll send a soldier to find you when we get back."

"We'd appreciate it, Major," Trapp said, standing up.

They left with Casey, who clapped them both on the back outside.

"If you fellas are in the saloon later, I'll buy you a drink."

"See you there," Fry said.

When Trapp and Fry came out the back gate, Trapp said, "Four more days. That gives Keller plenty of time."

"Maybe we shouldn't wait for him," Fry said. "Maybe we should make the first move."

"What if we're wrong?" Trapp asked. "What if he isn't working for Train?"

"Well," Fry said, "we'll just have to find out for sure."

"How do you propose we do that?" Trapp asked.

"The easy way," Fry said. "We'll ask him."

THIRTY-SIX

"What do you mean he's not here?" Fry asked.

The hotel clerk looked at Trapp and Fry and said, "I'm sorry, but the man did not check in here."

"Is there another place he could get a room?" Trapp asked.

"Uh, yeah, as a matter of fact," the clerk said, "there's a rooming house on the other end of town."

"They have a bathtub?"

"I suppose so."

"That's where he is," Fry said, banging his hand down on the desk.

Trapp closed his hand over Fry's forearm and pulled him away from the desk.

"After he gets a bath and a change of clothes, what's he going to want?"

"Same things we want," Fry said. "Some food and a drink."

236

"Let's go and get those things and maybe we'll run into him in the saloon."

"Not another incident in the saloon," Fry said. "The sheriff wouldn't be able to believe it."

"We might not have so much trouble," Trapp said. "Remember, we've got the military on our side."

They left the hotel and went to the small café, Maria's. They each ordered the same thing, steak and potatoes.

"I've been thinking about what you said."

"About what?" Trapp asked.

"About the military being on our side," Fry said. "Quanah's not stupid. When he realizes that we've escaped, is he gonna keep his camp where it is, or move it?"

Trapp's heart dropped as he realized that Fry was absolutely correct.

"Of course he'll move it," Trapp said. "Probably take my Sharps with him."

For the first time Fry realized that Trapp was hoping the soldiers would be able to recover the Sharps.

"What about buying another Sharps?" Fry asked.

"Where?"

"How about when we get back to the mountains?"

"You know, I've been thinking a lot about the mountains," Trapp said.

"What about them?"

"They will be the same, but what about the area around them? Will the plains be different? Will there be towns like this one where I remembered grassy fields? And what about the people?"

"Trapp, you'll find out about all that when we get there, so why worry about it now?"

Trapp stared at the younger man for a moment then said, "Yeah, I guess you're right."

They finished their dinner and headed over to the saloon for a beer. The bartender recognized them, but did not comment on the condition of their faces, which were still red from the sun. They took their beers to a table against a wall and both sat so they could see the rest of the room.

"Maybe we should go and talk to the sheriff," Trapp said. "Tell him what we suspect."

"Ah, he'd just think we were trying to cover ourselves in case of trouble. No, if something happens here, Trapp, we'll have plenty of witnesses afterward."

"That's supposing that we're both around afterward," Trapp said.

"Why shouldn't we be? I mean, I've heard that Keller is good, but there are two of us."

"You mean you'd have us both go against him at the same time?"

Fry stared at Trapp and asked, "Why not? If he comes in here looking for the both of us, it's his choice. Are we going to be gentlemen about it and say 'Here, Mr. Keller, face me first, and if you kill me, then you'll have to face my friend'? That doesn't make any sense, Trapp."

"It just . . . doesn't seem right."

After a moment Fry said, "Look, if it bothers you I'll take him alone."

"Can you?" Trapp said.

"Can I what? Take him? Sure."

"Have you ever seen him—I mean, you've never seen him before."

"Don't worry about it, Trapp," Fry said. "The important thing isn't having seen his move before, the important thing is having confidence in yourself."

"Which you obviously do," Trapp said. "How can you be so confident that you can outshoot everyone?"

"I can't outshoot *every*one," Fry said. "I'm not dumb enough to think that. Somewhere out there is a better hand than me with a gun. I just have to hope that he and I never find ourselves in the same place at the same time."

"And if it's Keller?"

Fry shrugged.

"If it's Keller and he kills me, you better get acquainted real quick with that new rifle of yours."

Trapp looked down at the Winchester leaning against the table.

"I don't even know if I could fire it now."

"Lift it up here," Fry said.

Trapp put the rifle on the table.

"It's a lever action. Just work the lever to load a round, and fire. Then you lever next time to eject the spent shell and load a live one. See?"

"It's simple," Trapp said, somewhat surprised.

"Much easier than having to reload that Sharps of yours every time you fire, isn't it."

"Yes, it is," Trapp said, touching the gun.

"Okay, get it off the table before we attract attention."

Trapp took the gun and leaned it against the table again.

"Now drink your beer and get used to waiting. Once we find him—or he finds us—we can flat out ask him if he's hunting us, but that could be in the next hour, or three days from now."

Keller got up off his bed in his room at the rooming house and strapped on his new gun. It was a piece of shit, but it was the best weapon the gunsmith had in his shop. When he got to a real town, he'd buy himself a brand new one. He liked the idea of going into retirement with a brand new weapon.

His intention now was to go to the saloon and get a beer. He knew that if there was one place in Fort McAdams that he'd be likely to run into Trapp and Kid Fry, it would be the saloon.

Unbeknownst to Trapp and Fry, Keller had heard that Sergeant Casey would be taking some wagons across the Staked Plains in four days' time. Keller figured that Trapp and Fry would wait and leave with the wagons. That gave him four days to play games with them and unnerve them. He wasn't sure yet if he wanted to take the two of them at one time. As a hand with a gun, he didn't anticipate much trouble from Trapp, although he was otherwise impressed with the man and the things he had done out on the plains.

Kid Fry, on the other hand, had a reputation as a hand with a gun. Keller knew he could handle a gun, but that was not where his reputation lay. His reputation was as a hunter of men. Rarely did he face a quarry fairly when he caught up with them. Not that he shot them in the back, but he didn't quite play fair with the boys who thought that standing out in the street and shooting it out fair and square was the measure of a man.

The measure of a man was in surviving and that is what Keller was good at—and the reason he was good at it was because he always survived . . . no matter what the cost.

THIRTY-SEVEN

They saw Keller as soon as he walked in.

He walked to the bar, got himself a beer, and looked around the room, apparently without seeing them. When he'd finished taking the room in, he pushed away from the bar and walked right over to their table.

He *had* seen them as soon as he'd walked in.

"You boys mind if I sit down?" he asked.

"I don't see why not," Fry said, "after all that we've been through together . . . Keller."

Keller smiled.

"I guess I should apologize for that little lie."

"I don't see why," Trapp said. "Wouldn't do for you to introduce yourself to a man you were hunting, would it? I mean, that's sure as hell not the way you've made your reputation in your business, is it?"

"No, it isn't," Keller said. "You know, I'm real sorry

242

that I am hunting you, because after what we went through together, none of us should have to kill the other."

"Then you admit that you're hunting both of us?" Fry asked.

"No," Keller said, and made them wait for clarification while he sipped his beer. "I'm hunting him." He pointed to Trapp, and was talking to Fry. "You just happen to be with him."

"And I ain't goin' away," Fry said.

"I didn't think you would."

"I suppose you've made arrangements to be compensated?" Fry said.

"Oh, yes," Keller said. "I've made all my arrangements—and now I'm giving you two time to make yours."

"I haven't got any arrangements to make, Keller," Trapp said. "I'm going to my mountain, remember?"

"I remember hearing something about that," Keller said, "but I'm here to tell you you ain't gonna make it."

"That's you talking," Trapp said.

"I usually mean what I say."

"So do I," Trapp said. He leaned closer to Keller, stared him in the eyes, and said, "Don't get between me and my mountain. I don't think I can make myself any clearer than that."

Keller held Trapp's eyes for a few moments, then looked at Fry.

"You know, if he was ten years younger—even *five* years—I'd be afraid, I surely would."

"Be afraid," Fry said. "You saw him out there, Keller. This ain't no normal man."

"Out there," Keller said, nodding. "Out there, I saw a man running on fear. Fear can make you do things you can't normally do."

Fry laughed.

"Fear? It was you and me running on fear, Keller. This man never showed an ounce of it, and you know why? Because he never felt it."

"Everybody feels fear," Keller said.

"I'm glad you said that, Keller," Trapp said.

"Why?"

"Because it tells me that you're not a stupid man. When you make your decision and it turns out to be the wrong one, I'll be glad to know that it wasn't based on stupidity."

Trapp put his hand on Keller's left forearm and closed it. Keller tried, but he couldn't move it from the table.

"I just figured out a way to be clearer," Trapp said urgently. "Don't get between me and my mountain, or I'll kill you."

He released Keller's arm, got up, and walked out of the saloon.

"He means it," Fry said.

Keller flexed his left hand to work the blood back into it and said, "I know it, but I've been paid to do a job, Fry, and I've never failed to complete one."

"There's always a first time," Fry said. "Why don't we just put that to the test now?"

"Now?" Keller asked. "I haven't finished my beer."

"I could wait for you outside."

"You'd be waiting a long time, Fry," Keller said. "No, I think I'll decide when we put that to the test. After all, I *am* the hunter."

"We could go to the sheriff."

"And tell him what? That I'm hunting you? He knows what happened to us out there. It's all over town. Everybody thinks we're good buddies. Besides, going to the law isn't your style, Fry, just like it isn't mine."

They both worked on their beers for a while and it was Keller who broke the silence.

"You know, you've got a pretty good reputation. If you stood back and let me take Trapp, you and I could then square off and find out who's better."

"Who are you kidding?"

Keller looked wounded and said, "What do you mean?"

"You ain't no gunman, Keller, you're a killer. A fair fight ain't your style."

Keller held up a finger warningly and said, "I never shot a man in the back."

"There are other ways to fight unfairly than shooting a man in the back," Fry said, standing up. "I'd hazard a guess that you've perfected almost all of them."

Keller stared at Fry and then laughed as the younger man walked away and out of the saloon.

They were more alike than young Fry knew.

When Fry left the saloon, he found Trapp standing outside.

"What happened after I left?" Trapp asked.

"I hope you don't think you scared him."

"Nah, just maybe made him think a little. Why, what did he say?"

"He said if I stood aside while he took you out, then he and I could see who the better man is."

"And what'd you say?"

"I told him he'd never fought a fair fight in his life, and I didn't expect him to start now."

"Can we prod him?"

"No," Fry said, shaking his head. "He's gonna make his move when he's ready, and not before."

"What makes him think he's got the time?"

"He must know about the wagons that are leaving at the end of the week," Fry said. "He don't have to be the smartest dog in the pack to figure out that we'll be leaving with them. Last thing we want to do is visit Quanah Parker again. I don't think he likes the way we left the last time."

"Probably not," Trapp said. "It *was* rude of us."

"To say the least."

"Well," Trapp said, "I'm going to turn in. I've had a rough day, for a man my age."

"*We've* had a rough day for a man any age," Fry said, "but I think I'll stay out here and watch Mr. Keller for a while."

"Why?"

Fry shrugged.

"You thinking of trying to scare him?"

"No," Fry said, "he won't scare for sure, but maybe I can make him think a little."

"Well, be careful," Trapp said, and started to walk away. He took two steps and turned back.

"What's the matter?"

"I just got a nasty little thought."

"About what?"

"You wouldn't be thinking of trying anything alone, would you?"

"And make you miss the fun?" Fry asked. "You'd never forgive me."

"You're right," Trapp said, "I wouldn't. Try to remember that."

"I'll remember it, Trapp," Fry said. "I'll remember it."

Trapp went back to the hotel, but he was uncomfortable about doing so. Fry may have had a little—or big—reputation, but he was still twenty-five years old. Trapp remembered being really headstrong at twenty-five, and although Fry had shown no signs of it yet, that didn't mean that it wasn't there.

Leaving him on the street alone may not be the right thing to do.

Fry watched Trapp walk away, then moved into the confines of a dark doorway to await Keller. Once Keller came out, Fry would let the man see him, and would follow him back to his rooming house. There would not even be an *implied* threat, but just the simple fact that Fry was there would have to make Keller think twice . . . and thinking twice was a hazard in his business.

As soon as Fry left the saloon, Keller got up and went to the bar and caught the bartender's attention.

"Another, sir?"

"No. Is there a back door out of here?"

"Yes, sir, right through that curtain and down the hall, but we don't allow customers . . . uh, sir? You can't go back there. Sir!"

THIRTY-EIGHT

Keller slipped out the back door, ignoring the words of the bartender. After all, the man had made no move to physically stop him. Smart man.

It was dark out and he stopped for a moment to allow his eyes to adjust, then began to move along the rear of the buildings until he came to an alley. He moved down the alley, came to the main street, and stopped. He peered around the corner and found that he was only one building away from the saloon. Across the street the doorways were dark, but he knew if he was patient—ah, there it was. Just enough movement to tell him that someone was there, in one of the doorways.

He wondered if it was Trapp or Fry. His money was on the younger man, Fry. Trapp would have more patience.

That *lack* of patience was going to get the young man killed.

* * *

Fry wondered how long he was going to have to wait. He'd be the first to admit that patience was not his long suit. Maybe that was something he could learn from Trapp. The older man had really impressed him out on the plains. He wondered what kind of man John Henry Trapp was twenty-five years ago.

He would like to have met him then.

Keller eased himself out of the alley, keeping to the sides of the buildings, where the shadows were deep. Somebody would actually have to be looking for him to see him. Fry was probably waiting for him to come out the front door so he could tail him. He probably felt that he'd unnerve Keller by doing that. It was the kind of foolish decision a young man would make.

Keller moved carefully, so he wouldn't bump into anything and give himself away.

He knew what doorway Fry was in. All he had to do was get himself into position to make his shots count. If he put two or three into that doorway, he was sure to hit his target.

There was plenty of moonlight, which lit the center of the street, but it was that very moonlight that made the shadows black as ink.

Finally he slid into a doorway which gave him an excellent vantage point of the other doorway across the street. He settled in and waited. He wanted one more indication that he had the correct target.

He waited and waited but there was no movement. Either Fry had suddenly become very, very still . . . or he was no longer there. If he had moved, firing a shot into the doorway would only give away his own position.

Maybe the young man was better than he thought.

It was quite by accident that Fry saw the movement across the street. He had looked away from the saloon entrance for a moment, just long enough for his eyes to adjust to the shadows. He caught some movement, as if someone was moving in the shadows across the street.

The back way, he thought. Keller had probably used the saloon's back exit to get out.

It looked as if they both had the same idea, to make something happen tonight.

As quickly and quietly as he could, he slipped from his doorway and moved farther down, away from the saloon. He found an alley and took refuge in it, peering around the edge.

Now he'd *have* to show some patience, or end up dead.

Keller decided to retrace his steps, going back down the alley and moving along the rear of the buildings until he was farther down the street, where he could safely cross without being seen.

Once on the other side he found another alley, which led him to the rear of the buildings on that side of the street. He now felt confident that he was *behind* Fry.

All he had to do now was find him.

* * *

Fry knew that Keller had moved—but where would he have moved to? He decided that there were two options. The man had either gone to the rooftops, or had somehow crossed the street and was now on the same side.

Suddenly he looked behind himself, into the darkness of the alley. Keller could be moving in behind him.

Now he had a tough choice to make. He could move farther into the alley and risk running right into Keller, or he could slip out of the alley and take a chance on exposing himself.

Although it was dark it was still early enough for there to be *some* street traffic. Every so often a man, or two men—sometimes soldiers—would pass by. Fry wondered if and when the sheriff made his rounds. He could always ask the man for help, but somehow that went against his grain. He was used to taking care of his own problems.

Gun in hand, he decided to risk moving deeper into the alley.

Keller was moving along behind the buildings, and every time he came to an alley, he peered into it. At the end of each alley he could see the moonlit street. If there was someone in the alley, he kept to the side of the building on either side.

He gave each alley a few minutes, then passed it and moved on to the next, always keeping a sharp eye behind him.

He was approaching the third alleyway when someone came out of it, moving slowly.

It had to be Fry.

Keller raised his gun and fired.

Fry felt the impact before he heard the shot—or at least, that was the way he remembered it.

The bullet hit him in the hip and spun him around, but he held on to his gun and squeezed off a shot, just for the scare value of the noise. When he hit the ground, he scrambled and crawled until he found cover behind some crates.

Keller knew he had hit his target, but there was a flash and a shot as Fry pulled his trigger, and Keller hit the ground. He heard some scrabbling on the ground and correctly deduced that Fry was crawling to cover.

"I know I hit you, Fry," he said. "I can smell the blood. As of now, as you run out of blood, you run out of time." He paused then said loudly, "I'm gonna kill you, Fry."

Keller knew that it would take time for anyone to figure out where the shots had come from. There had been only two and they were close together. Some people—especially those in the saloon—would still be listening, to make sure they had heard right.

He had time to make his killing shot.

Fry was trying to stop the bleeding.

He knew the wound wasn't serious, but he had to stop the bleeding or he'd be in big trouble. He pulled his shirt out of his pants, tore off a large piece of it, and wadded it up. He unbuttoned his pants and slid the wadded cloth in until it covered the wound, then he buttoned the pants again. That would slow down the bleeding—unless he had to move.

He knew that Keller was right. Where they both once had time and mobility on their side, he now had neither. Keller could wait or move, at his leisure—unless the shots brought somebody, which wasn't likely. He made the same assumptions that Keller made about the shots being too close together and difficult to pinpoint.

Of course, if there were *more* shots . . .

When the shots came, Keller ducked, but then realized that Fry was not shooting at him. The kid was firing to bring help.

Keller knew that he had to move fast now. He stood up and moved quickly toward Fry, who now fired another shot in the air.

He had two shots left.

Too late, Fry realized how Keller would respond to his shots. He turned too quickly, pain lancing through his hip. He put his left hand down on the ground to brace himself and it slid on the sticky blood. Keller was moving toward him fast, and as Fry raised his gun to fire, Keller kicked out. His foot struck Fry's hand and the gun went flying.

Keller was standing over him, his gun pointing down at him.

"Like I said before," Keller said, "it's too bad I have to do this, after we saved each other's lives from Quanah Parker."

"I can see you're real upset about it."

Keller smiled and cocked his gun.

"Keller!"

It was Trapp's voice. Both Keller and Fry looked around and finally saw Trapp, standing ahead of them. Fry wished Trapp had come up behind Keller.

"You're next, Trapp," Keller said. "Just let me finish here."

"I'm first, Keller," Trapp said. He had already left the hotel and was looking for Fry when he heard the shots. Even so, it wasn't until the second volley that he was able to pinpoint their location. "You've got to kill me before you can kill him."

Keller looked down at Fry. If he shot Fry, Trapp would shoot him. His only chance was to get Trapp first.

Trapp was holding his rifle in front of him, not pointing at Keller. Fry hoped that he had already levered in a round.

"Your call, Trapp," Keller said.

Keller started to bring the gun up, shifting his feet at the same time. He stepped in a sticky, slippery patch of Fry's blood and his foot slipped. As he was trying to regain his balance, Trapp shot him.

The bullet struck Keller squarely in the chest. Fry heard Trapp lever another round, but it wasn't needed. Keller's gun fell from his hand and the man-hunter toppled over onto his back.

Trapp moved forward as they heard some people coming down the alley.

"What's going on—" the sheriff demanded, coming into view. He saw Trapp and Fry and said, "Oh no, not you two again."

Trapp ignored the lawman and crouched down by Fry.

"Are you all right?"

"I am now," Fry said. "I'm glad you remembered how to use that rifle."

"So am I. Can you stand?"

"I think so."

Trapp helped him to his feet and supported him.

"This one's dead," the sheriff said, crouched by Keller. He stood up and said, "You two want to explain this to me?"

"As soon as we get my partner to a doctor, Sheriff," Trapp promised, "I'll tell you the whole story."

EPILOGUE

Three Months Later

"What do you think?" Trapp asked.

Kid Fry looked up at the majestic Rocky Mountains and said, "Is that snow?"

"It's snow, Kid," Trapp said.

"White as pearls," Fry said, remembering what Trapp had said.

Fry winced and Trapp said, "How's the hip?"

"Sore," Fry said. "The doc said riding would do that to it for a while—maybe forever."

"Well, you're lucky that bullet lodged in your hip, or it would have tore a bigger hole going out and you'd have been laid up even longer."

The rest of the trip, after leaving Texas, had been uneventful for the most part. Of course, they'd crossed paths once or twice with trouble, but never with the same result as in Texas. Sometimes Trapp thought that if they had been able to avoid crossing Texas, the trip would have been faster and easier—and certainly less painful.

Trapp hefted the weight of his Sharps, wondering when they'd catch their first sight of buffalo—or if there were even any buffalo left, or beaver.

Crossing the plains at the foot of the mountains, he had already seen the changes he'd been afraid of. Settlements, even the beginnings of real towns. Already there were too damn many people around.

Up top, though, that's where he felt it would be the same.

"Up there," he said, pointing. "When we get up there, we won't have to worry about people, about anybody."

"That'll be a nice change."

Trapp looked down at his Sharps. He'd gotten it back the day after the shooting, when the major returned from his search for Quanah's camp. . . .

The soldier had had mixed luck. They had found the camp and killed themselves some Indians—among them, Trapp was quite sure, some women and children—but Quanah and his warriors had not been there.

"Not your fault, Mr. Trapp," the major said magnanimously. "Even though we didn't get Quanah, we hurt him. Maybe it'll make him think twice about showing his face again for a while."

"Well," Trapp said, thinking of the little black-eyed son of Strong Hawk, "that's something, isn't it?"

"We did find something you might be interested in, though," the major said. "Sergeant Casey?"

Casey came running over then, and in his hand he was carrying Trapp's Sharps.

"Well, I'll be—" Trapp said, grabbing for it.

"I don't think they even knew how to work it," the major said. "It's a beautiful old weapon. I thought you might like to have it back."

"Thank you, Major," Trapp said. "This means a lot to me."

When Fry was ready to ride, they had hit the trail again, and now, finally, they were here.

Trapp was home again.

The air was the same, clean, fresh, and cold enough to freeze your piss.

They came to a stream and Trapp made Fry drink the water.

"Oh, my God," Fry said after sipping some, "that's the coldest thing I ever drank."

"How do you like it?"

"It's also the best thing I ever drank," Fry said. "Do you know how beer would taste if you put it in a barrel and dropped it in there?"

"Delicious," Trapp said. "Delicious."

At that point a Blackfoot party had come along and chased them across the stream halfheartedly. After a couple of hundred yards the Indians gave up the chase. They probably could have run them down if they'd really wanted to, but back in one of those plains settlements they had already picked up a pack horse and extra supplies.

"After the Comanches," Fry said, "that was easy as pie."

"Take it from me," Trapp said, "they're not always that friendly."

They camped that night just below the snow peaks. In the morning they'd go up higher, where Trapp wanted to be for a while. He wanted to wash all the poison of the past twenty-five years out of his system, and the only way he knew to do that was to get as high as a man could get without flying.

They made bacon, and some coffee, and Trapp looked across the fire at Kid Fry.

"Before I take you up there," Trapp said, jerking his chin upward, "up to my mountain, I want to know something from you."

"What?" Fry asked warily.

"What are you running from?"

Fry stared at Trapp, then looked up at the snow peaks that looked as if they were getting ready to poke holes in the sky.

"I was gonna tell you, Trapp," Fry said. "I think I was gonna tell you up there."

"Well, tell me down here, Kid," Trapp said. "Tell me now."

"It's no big deal, really," Fry said. "I just fudged a bit on my reputation."

"How little?"

"Well, you asked me if I'm wanted by the law. Fact of the matter is, I am. There's probably paper on me reaching Texas and Oklahoma right now."

"Paper?"

"Wanted posters."

"From where?"

"New Mexico. You see, my reputation isn't all that small, and I've been trying to get away from it of late. But it seemed that in the three or four months before I met you, I was being challenged more and more. Every time I came out of a hotel or a saloon, there was somebody there wanting to try me out."

Trapp remained silent when Fry paused, and waited for him to continue.

"Well, I was in a town in New Mexico, having a drink in a saloon. It was late, and I guess I'd had one or two too many. I came out of the saloon and suddenly somebody called my name, real loud. I reacted instinctively. I turned and fired, all in one motion."

This time when Fry paused, Trapp became impatient.

"And?"

"And . . . it was a kid," Fry said. "Fourteen, and he had no gun."

"He was dead?"

"Dead," Fry said. "I killed an unarmed kid just because he called my name."

"What happened after that?"

"Well, people started pouring out of the saloon and when they saw what I'd done they started some lynch talk right away. I don't mind telling you, I ran. I was running when we met, and I'm still running."

"That was why you never wanted to use your name on telegrams, or talk to a lawman?"

Fry nodded.

"It takes paper some time to circulate, but I was playing it safe," Fry said. "You'll recall I wanted to leave Texas earlier than we finally did."

"You would have killed yourself, trying to ride on that wound."

"Yeah, I might have," Fry said, "but I was afraid that paper would catch up with us."

"Well," Trapp said, "it won't catch up to you up there."

Fry looked at Trapp and said, "You'll still take me, even though you know I'm wanted?"

Trapp shrugged.

"You forget, I'm wanted, too," Trapp said. "When Sam Train finds out that we killed Keller, you don't think he's going to quit, do you? He'll send somebody else."

"And he'll send them here," Fry said. "It won't be hard for him to figure that you'd come back here, to the mountains."

"Well, also don't forget," Trapp said, "this is my mountain. I know every inch of it, and the terrain will be unchanged even after twenty-five years. Nobody will find us up here, or up there, Kid. It'll just be you and me."

"You, me," Fry said, "and our pasts."

"Well," Trapp said, "what do you say we leave our pasts down here and only take our futures up there."

Trapp stuck his hand out and Fry smiled and took it.

"Just one thing," Fry said.

"What?"

"I don't know what we'll do with our time up there, but just don't ask me to play poker with you."

WILL COOK

UNTIL DAY BREAKS

North Texas, 1870. For three years a delicate peace has existed between the U.S. Army and the Comanche, led by Quanah Parker. The architect of this peace, General Tracy Cameron, has given an impassioned speech in Washington to plead for continued peace with the Plains Indians. His aide, Second Lieutenant Jim Gary, has been assigned to persuade General William T. Sherman that his plan for a military attack on the Comanche would be a deadly error. Meanwhile, Quanah Parker is organizing the Kiowa and Cheyenne to join him in an effort to drive the white buffalo hunters from the plains. As each side forms battle plans, a spark is all that is needed to ignite the frontier into total war!

WALT COBURN

BORDER WOLVES

This exciting volume collects three of Walt Coburn's finest short novels, two of which have been made into classic Western movies. "Rusty Rides Alone," a thrilling tale of a brutal range war, became the film of the same name, starring Tim McCoy. "The Block K Rides Tonight" is the story of Cole Griffin, who returns to Montana intent on finding the man who hanged his father years before. This story was filmed as *The Return of Wild Bill*, starring Bill Elliott. And "Border Wolves" draws on Coburn's own experiences as part of Pancho Villa's so-called "Gringo Battalion." Coburn paints the West not as it existed in legend or imagination, but as it really was.

Dorchester Publishing Co., Inc.
P.O. Box 6640
Wayne, PA 19087-8640

___5368-3
$4.99 US/$6.99 CAN

Please add $2.50 for shipping and handling for the first book and $.75 for each additional book. NY and PA residents, add appropriate sales tax. No cash, stamps, or CODs. Canadian orders require an extra $2.00 for shipping and handling and must be paid in U.S. dollars. Prices and availability subject to change. **Payment must accompany all orders.**

Name: _____

Address: _____

City: _____ State: _____ Zip: _____

E-mail: _____

I have enclosed $_____ in payment for the checked book(s).

CHECK OUT OUR WEBSITE! www.dorchesterpub.com
____ Please send me a free catalog.

A TRAIL TO WOUNDED KNEE

TIM CHAMPLIN

In 1876 tensions run high on the prairie, where settlers push ever westward into Indian territories. Lt. Thaddeus Coyle is supposed to help keep the peace. Little does he know the greatest threat is from his commanding officer. Driven to disobey a direct order, Coyle winds up court-martialed and abandoned by his family. A ruined man, he finds his only friend is Tom Merritt—also known as Swift Hawk—a Lakota caught between his heritage and the white man's world. But when Coyle gets a job as U.S. Special Indian Agent and is sent to Wounded Knee, he and Swift Hawk will find themselves on opposite sides of the law on a prairie ready to go up in flames at the slightest spark.